DRIFTER
PART ONE

A SAM PRICHARD MYSTERY

DRIFTER

PART ONE

DAVID ARCHER

USA TODAY BESTSELLING AUTHOR

"...THE NEXT JACK REACHER!"

PROLOGUE

"Daddy," Kenzie said as she twirled noodles onto her fork, "is that bad man dead, now?"

He'd known the question would be coming, because the little girl had been terrified when Darrel Unger, the serial killer who had challenged Sam to catch and stop him, had come into her mother's hospital room and threatened them all. Sam looked over at his wife, Indie; they'd decided to wait and let Kenzie bring it up, rather than trying to explain it to her before she was ready to hear it.

"Yes, Sweetie, he is," Sam said. "Did he scare you pretty bad?"

Kenzie sat there for a moment, twirling the fork, and then she set it down. "Yesterday," she said, "at children's church, they told us about God, and how when you're in trouble you should always ask God to help you. When that bad man came in and everyone got scared, I closed my eyes and asked God to help us, and He did."

Sam and Indie shared a glance, and Indie asked, "He did?"

Kenzie nodded her head. "Yes," she said. "I said, 'God, help us, cause there's a bad man and he wants to hurt us,' and then Daddy came back in and I knew God sent Daddy back to make sure the bad man didn't hurt anybody. But when you were talking to him, and he said he wanted to be dead, I knew God was gonna make him be dead, too, so he wouldn't hurt anyone anymore." She picked up her fork and took a big bite of spaghetti. "This is good, Daddy," she said, and then went on eating.

Sam and Indie looked at each other, and Sam asked the question they were both thinking. "Do you think it's time we started going to church regularly?"

Indie smiled. "I did sort of like it there," she said. "Caleb's a pretty good preacher."

They finished dinner and went to watch another movie—this one was an older movie about a pro football player who found out he was the father of a six-year-old girl when she showed up at his apartment with a note telling him her mother had to go out of the country, and it was time for him to take care of his child—and it was so delightful that even Indie was laughing in spots, with sort of a, "haha, *ow,* haha," pattern to it.

After that movie, Sam declared bedtime, and not even Kenzie argued. Because her Mommy was hurt, she let Sam go up and tuck her in, and by the time he got the story read and the lights out, Indie was in their bed and sound asleep. Sam crawled in beside her and put an arm around her as she slept, and it wasn't long before he felt the arms of sleep coming to cuddle him, as well.

Morning came, and for once he woke before she did. He slipped out of bed and took his shower, found her still sleeping when he was finished, and went out to put coffee on. While he drank his first cup, he sat down at the table and started going through all the phone messages from the night before.

Most of them, as he'd known they would be, were from reporters. He made notes of the few he would be willing to talk to, deleted the rest, and then came across one message that caught his attention. It had been the last call of the night, and had come in after they had all gone to bed.

"*Mr. Prichard,*" a woman's voice began, "*my name is Joellyn Finer. I'm calling because I've been told that you're the best Private Investigator in the area, and I've got a problem I need solved. It's probably not something you're used to dealing with, though, so I'll be brief, and I hope you'll call me back. You see, I never met my father, and I know very little about him, because he disappeared during the Vietnam war. Everyone thought he was dead, but I've just heard from someone who knew him that he's turned up alive, and I would like to hire you to find him and find out why I've never met him. If you'd call me back, I'd really appreciate it...*"

1

Most private investigators never have to deal with serial killers, no matter what the novelists say. Sam Prichard wasn't most private investigators, however, and just the previous week had seen him doing exactly that. The strange case had been thrust upon him and had almost cost him his life, and the life of his wife, Indie. It had finally ended with a showdown that required Sam to outwit the man, saving his entire family in the bargain.

Indie had been wounded, grazed across her head by a bullet that had been meant to kill her, and it had taken a few days for her to get back to normal, but she was finally there. Sam had been checking phone messages, keeping track of potential cases and automatically dismissing any that involved following unfaithful wives or husbands, or trying to trap people into doing something wrong. There had been one call the day after Indie had been released from the hospital, though, that had caught his attention, and it was time to learn more about it.

Sam and Indie were in the office, working on their quarterly business reports, when the day's first (and only) appointment showed up. The woman who parked beside the sign that read *Sam Prichard, Private Eye* was dressed casually, but there was something that seemed elegant about her, as she entered through the office door with a smile on her face.

Indie looked up and did a double take, then found her manners. "Hello," she said. "I'm Indiana Prichard, and this is my husband, Sam. I didn't mean to stare, but did you know you look a lot like Jennifer Aniston?"

The woman laughed. "Yeah, I hear that a lot," she said. "I've actually been one of her stunt doubles; back in twenty ten, she did a movie called *The Bounty Hunter,* and I was the one who got tossed out a window for her. I was hoping it would turn into a career, but it didn't, so now I'm in the catering business."

Indie smiled. "Catering is good, too," she said. "I always thought I'd want to do that, if I could cook."

"Don't believe her," Sam said as he rose to his feet and extended a hand. "She's a wonderful cook; she just likes keeping it in the family, and I'm in favor of that, too. I'm Sam Prichard, and I'm guessing that you're Joellyn Finer."

Joellyn shook his hand and nodded. "I am, and I'm glad to meet you. I've heard a lot of good things about you, and of course the newspapers are sort of full of your name, right now. The more I read about how you caught a serial killer that no one even knew was out there, the more sure I am that you're the man I need to talk to."

"Well, have a seat," Indie said, "and tell us how we can help you."

Joellyn sat down in the chair Indie had pointed to. "So, as I said the other day, I've been told that my father has shown up here in the area. He disappeared in Vietnam, you see, right after I was born, and I never met him; now, my uncle—his brother—says he turned up last month to come and visit their mother, my grandma, who's dying of COPD. He walked into her house like he'd never been gone, acting like nothing was out of the ordinary, until Uncle Jim got in his face, and then he said there was very little he could tell them about where he'd been for all these years. A little while later, he left, but he's been back a couple of times since."

"That sounds like he isn't really trying to hide, then," Indie said, but Joellyn shook her head.

"I tried hanging out at my grandma's place to see if I could meet him," she said, "but he won't show up if I'm there. I even tried hiding my car somewhere else and sneaking in the back door, but he still seems to know and won't show up. The only time he turns up is when no one but Grandma and Uncle Jim are there." She sighed, and looked at her hands. "I want to know where he's been, and I want to know why he never came back to my mom and me, if he was still alive. Everyone thought he was dead, you see, and this has been a real shock. My mother refuses to believe it's really him, but Uncle Jim says there's no doubt; I just need to know, Mr. Prichard, and I want you to find him and make him talk to me."

Sam sat there for a moment, thinking about it. "Ms. Finer," he said, "I might be able to find your father, if it really is him; however, that doesn't mean I can get him to talk to you. Unless he's done something illegal or is wanted in connection with a crime, I can't actually force him to do anything. And while I think running out on his family is a pretty despicable thing to do, it's not a crime."

Joellyn nodded. "I know," she said. "I guess I really just want you to find him, and tell me how I can go to him. If he still won't talk to me, then I'll deal with it somehow."

Sam looked at her, then glanced at his wife. Indie nodded, and he turned back to the client. "I charge a thousand as a retainer, and I get two fifty a day plus any expenses I have to lay out. I'm confident I can find him, but what happens after that is up to you and him. Deal?"

Joellyn smiled. "Deal. Is cash okay?"

Sam grinned. "Legal tender, they call it," he said as Indie made out a receipt and took the money. "Now, tell me what you can about your father and uncle."

"Well, my father's name is Kenneth Long; Finer is my married name, even though I'm divorced, now. He was born January fourth, nineteen forty-nine. He grew

7

up in Denver, played basketball in high school. He married his high school sweetheart, my mother Margaret Wilkins Long, in nineteen sixty-seven, and joined the army a month later. In August of sixty-eight he was deployed to Vietnam, and spent seven months there on active duty. On March fifteenth of sixty-nine, he went out on a patrol with his squad, and only a few of them were ever seen again, until he walked into my grandma's house last month. Some of them turned up as POWs and were released at the end of the war."

Sam cocked his head. "Was he ever declared dead by the Army?"

"No, he was MIA, and because there were no reports of any fighting near where he disappeared, and the rest of the patrol was found as POWs, either alive or dead, it was assumed that he was also captured, so he was left on MIA status. That meant that my mom kept getting his pay and allowances, and she still gets them. As long as there's the slightest possibility that he's alive and not a deserter, they said, she keeps getting his pay."

Sam grunted. "If he's running around the USA, then I'd have to say it's highly unlikely he's been a POW all this time. Sounds to me like your mother has a vested interest in it not being him; if it is, the government may want her to pay back all that money."

Joellyn frowned. "That hadn't occurred to me, but I guess it's a possibility. My biggest concern is finding out why I haven't heard from him before now, why he never came back to us or even got in touch."

"There are a lot of stories about MIAs and POWs turning up alive, and at least some of them have some basis in truth. I remember one just a couple of years ago, a Sergeant Robinson, who claimed to have been captured and held prisoner for years, then escaped and started a new life with a woman who rescued him. It was a big fuss, but then a few days later, it came out that it was a hoax, and the long-lost soldier was a Vietnamese man who had been trying to pass himself off as an MIA for years. In other cases, it turned out they were never captured at all, but had either taken their discharge there and stayed, or deserted and stayed. Your father sounds like he might fit the latter category."

Joellyn shrugged. "I can't disagree with you, but I admit I'd like to know. What else can I tell you?"

"You say it's your uncle who's seen him most?" Sam asked.

"Yes. He's seen him at my grandma's house four times, now. I asked him to tell him I want to see him, but he said my father only shakes his head and walks away when he mentions me. Uncle Jim, that's James Long, he says the only thing my father will tell them is that he was a prisoner for a couple of years, and then after he was rescued, he said he was recruited by the CIA to stay there and work for the government as a spy. If that's true, then maybe he won't be in so much trouble after all. Like I said, none of that actually matters to me;

I just want to look him in the eye and find out why I grew up without a father."

Sam sighed. "Okay, I'm going to need all the information you can give me on your father, your uncle, your mother and grandmother, everyone connected to this. I'll find him if it's possible, and tell you if it isn't."

The three of them sat and talked, and Indie made notes, writing down everything Joellyn said that related to her father or the case in any way. Sam made sure they got addresses and phone numbers for everyone that they could, knowing the magic that Indie could work through the internet when it came to tracking people down. They got everything they could think of, told Joellyn they'd be in touch if they needed anything else, and said goodbye as she left.

"I'll get Herman on this, see if there's any info he can find on Mr. Long," Indie said. "You're gonna start with his brother?"

Sam nodded. "That's what I'm thinking, yeah. If good old Uncle Jim can't tell her anything, though, then he won't have anything to tell me, either, so there's no point wasting time asking questions. I think we'll see what I can find out by just keeping an eye on him. If Daddy doesn't know I'm watching, then he shouldn't have a reason to hide, right?"

"Right," Indie said, "but if you talk to the uncle first, and he mentions to Daddy that there's a PI looking for him..."

"Exactly. Then he disappears into the woodwork like a cockroach when the light comes on."

Indie looked closely at Sam. "Something about this case is really bugging you, isn't it?" she asked, and after a moment's hesitation, he nodded.

"Yeah," he said. "I'm trying to get myself into the mind of a man who has a family, but either runs out on them, or doesn't do everything he can to get back to them when he gets the chance. If he just bugged out and decided not to come home, I wanna know why—but if he really was captured, and then didn't come home when he finally got rescued or escaped, then I want to know what the hell is wrong with him, what did they do to him that would make him refuse to come home to his wife and daughter?" He ran a hand over his face, and then looked Indie in the eye. "I've got you and Kenzie," he said, "and if something took me away from you for a long time, I'd spend every waking moment trying to escape and get back to you, and if I managed to get free, there is nothing on earth that would keep me from coming home."

Indie smiled and reached over to touch his hand. "I know," she said. "And I want you to know that if anything ever did happen to you, I'd never give up believing you were coming back, unless they showed me your dead body—and I'm not sure even that would stop you!" She added the last part with a wink, and both of them laughed.

"Yeah, well," Sam said. "Me and Death have been getting to know each other a lot better than I like, lately. I can't say he's a guy I really like hanging out with, though, so if he ever wants to come for me, he'd better bring help!"

Indie squeezed his hand. "Okay, then," she said, "let's see what Herman can find out about this guy. What should I put in the filters?"

Sam thought about it for a moment. "Well, we've got his name, date of birth, and the date of his disappearance, so let's begin with those. I wish we had the names of the other men who disappeared with him; there might be more of the missing ones who have turned up alive, if he did."

Indie smiled and tapped at her keyboard. "Let me have Herman search the news stories around that date, and we might find them. With a little effort, I think I can get you anything you want on those guys, all of 'em. What else?"

"Let's just go with that, for starters, and I'm gonna do a little old-fashioned detective work on the phone. There's one guy I can think of who might be able to help me get a line on this clown, and I haven't talked to him in a few days."

Indie was nodding, a big smile on her face. "Harry Winslow," she said. "Tell the old codger I said hi, please."

Sam grinned and took his phone out of his pocket,

then tapped the icon he'd put in to identify Harry's number—a cartoon picture of Elmer Fudd. He heard ringing on the other end, and then the southern drawl of Harry Winslow answered the phone.

"Sam, boy," the old man said with a smile in his voice, "to what earth-shattering disaster do I owe the pleasure of this call?"

"Harry, now, that hurts," Sam said. "You're implying that I only call you when there's something wrong, or when I need something. Can't I just call up and say hi to an old friend?"

There was a chuckle on the other end. "Well, of course you can," Harry said, "but the question is, will you? Never mind that, Sam, how's that lovely wife of yours? Headaches all gone, now? Except for the ones she gets from you, I mean?"

Sam grinned. "She says she's back to normal, and sends her love to you. As for the headaches, I don't think those will ever go away completely as long as we're in this business."

"Probably true," Harry said. "So, what's the headache that has you calling an old man during his lunch break?"

Sam glanced at the time on his phone and saw that it was only half past ten. "Lunch break?" he asked. "They got you on a different schedule than the rest of us, huh? I don't get lunch for another two hours or so."

"Yes, but you didn't get awakened at four AM by a frantic technician who thought that a message from DC that made reference to a party this coming week was a coded message for my eyes only. He's spending the next two weeks in some intensive training in non-classified message protocols, and I'm at Red Lobster. Care to come and join me?"

"Another time, maybe," Sam said. "Right now, I do have a question for you. I've just taken on a case involving a man who went missing back in nineteen sixty-nine in Vietnam. He was never declared dead, just kept on the MIA rosters all this time, and now he may have turned up alive here in the city, claiming that he's been working for Uncle Sam over there ever since he was released from a VC prison camp. I'm wondering if you think there could be any truth to the story."

"Well, Sam," Harry said. "I've heard of such stories before, and it's possible there could be some truth to some of them. I know that a lot of men who never were accounted for simply chose to stay there, though."

"Yeah, I know about some of those," Sam said, "and the cases of people claiming to be former POWs who really weren't. The thing about this one is that the guy showed up here when his mother took sick, but he refuses to see his wife and daughter, who is my client. How can I find out if he's for real, Harry?"

"Got a name?"

"Kenneth Long," Sam said. "Date of birth oh one, oh four, forty-nine; went missing on patrol in Vietnam on oh three, fifteen, sixty-nine."

"The Ides of March," Harry said. "Give me half an hour and I'll get you what I can."

As always when Sam was talking to Harry, the line went dead without another word, and he turned back to Indie. "He's gonna do some digging, too. Herman find anything?"

"He found the news story from when Long and his buddies disappeared," she said with a grin. "Listen to this: March seventeenth, nineteen sixty-nine. Seven American GIs are listed as missing in action after their patrol failed to report back to its designated unit on Saturday. Military sources say the patrol was a routine measure to observe and report on North Vietnamese troop activities in the region, which was only a few miles south of the demilitarized zone. Despite an intense search of the area of the patrol, there have been no signs found of any firefights, and no sign of bodies or injuries. According to Captain John Morris, their commanding officer, it was as if the men were simply taken by the darkness, leaving no sign that they were ever there. The missing men are listed as Second Lieutenant Charles Martin, twenty-six; Staff Sergeant Michael Bull, twenty-nine; Corporal Kenneth Long, twenty; PFC William Shine, twenty; PFC Gary McCall, twenty; PVT James Murdock, nineteen; and PVT Aaron Beasley, nineteen." She looked up at him. "I've already got Herman running each of them through every military database I can get into. If there's any information on them, even just that their remains were identified, he'll find it."

Sam leaned over and kissed her. "You do realize that Herman is half the reason I married you, right?"

Indie giggled. "Yeah, but he can't do some of the things you like most about me!"

"That's true," Sam said, and kissed her again. "I noticed that Long was a corporal in that patrol, so he was in the chain of command. I'd love to hear what actually happened that night; strikes me as pretty odd that there would be no signs of any kind of struggle, but a seven-man patrol disappears completely. That sounds almost impossible, but apparently it happened."

"Just got a hit," Indie said. "James Murdock. He was a private in that patrol, and was recovered in Operation Homecoming in nineteen seventy-three. He claimed that the patrol was captured without a shot being fired, when Lieutenant Martin was suddenly overtaken by a number of VC, and he ordered everyone to surrender. According to his account, two of the men refused and ran off into the surrounding jungle; one was PFC Gary McCall, and I bet you can't guess who the other one was."

"Long, no doubt," Sam said. "Interesting; he didn't fight, but refused to surrender. Anything else?"

Indie nodded. "Yeah, he says he saw McCall again a couple of days later, when they were taken to a holding facility on the way to a prison in Hanoi. McCall told him he'd been wounded by enemy fire as they ran off, and was captured the next morning. Long had escaped, and was planning to try a rescue, he said, but they never saw him again and assumed he was dead. Some of the others died while they were in the prison, including the lieutenant and Sergeant Bull. As far as Murdock knew, only he, McCall and Beasley survived."

Sam shook his head. "If Long was never captured, then I wonder where he was all that time. Of course, he might have been captured at a later date, or taken to a different prison. I wonder if Murdock might be available and willing to talk to me."

Indie shrugged and smiled. "Had a feeling you'd want it, so I tracked down his address and phone number. He lives in North Carolina, and he's almost sixty-six, now." She scribbled something down on a scrap of paper and handed it to him.

Sam looked at it for a moment, and then took out his phone, but before he could dial the number, it rang. Sam glanced at it, then mouthed, "It's Harry," and answered it.

"That wasn't a half hour," he said.

"Sue me," Harry answered. "Here's what I've got for you, Boy. Your guy was listed MIA, even though some of the men from his patrol were later identified as POWs. He may be a spook of some kind, but if he is, it's so covered up in red tape and BS that I can't cut through it quickly. He's still listed as MIA from the Nam, and his wife is collecting his pay, never has made any effort to have him declared dead. Could be she knows something, but maybe she's just not interested in being single again. Lot of MIA wives kept getting the hubby's pay, and just shacked up with a new guy if one came along."

"So there's nothing you can find that indicates he's telling the truth? Indie found a reference in the news that indicates he may never have been captured at all, or at least not when the records say he was."

Harry laughed. "Son, I can't find anything says he was captured; just missing. For all I know, he might have been on CIA payroll when he went over there; you'd be shocked how many recruit soldiers were turned into assassins before they ever got out of training. They were sent over and into normal units with special orders that superseded any that came from their commanding officers, and their COs knew it. They were attached to a regular infantry or artillery unit, but answered to the CIA handler who would come and visit periodically. That often created some interesting problems for their commanders."

"I can imagine that it did," Sam said. "But what would that have to do with him disappearing into the woodwork for so many years?"

"Sam, boy," Harry said, "that's the kind of question that often got people killed back in those days. In fact, I'm not sure you should be asking any questions at all about this guy. However, since I know you, I'm sure that's not gonna slow you down. The only thing I can do in this case is offer you some advice, and you know what advice is worth, right?"

"It's worth exactly what you pay for it," Sam said. "Go ahead, Harry, I'm listening."

"Sam, the smartest thing you can do with this case is to run from it. As far as you can and as fast as you can. That's the best advice I can give you at this time. Now, having said that, and knowing that you're not gonna listen, I'm going to offer you the second-best advice I can. Be sure you keep a gun handy, and do not, I repeat, do not, let that man get behind you. If he's one of the assassins that we sent over there, he's not a man even I would want to face in a dark alley."

"Okay, Harry," Sam said. "Can you imagine any reason one of those people would be showing up now, running around loose here in Denver?"

"Sam, I wouldn't have the slightest idea what could bring one of them back home, if they hadn't come back on their own years ago. That's why I'm saying not to let the guy get behind you; something about this is bugging me, and I don't know enough to put a finger on it. I'm hoping you're gonna keep in close touch with me on this one, son."

"I've got a feeling you can count on it, Harry."

2

Sam hung up the phone, then sat and looked at it for a long minute. Indie stayed quiet, waiting for him to be ready to say whatever was on his mind. She knew him, and knew that he would; he always shared his thoughts with her when he was ready.

"Harry thinks Kenneth Long may be more of a problem than we anticipated. It could very well be that he was some sort of government assassin back in the Vietnam era. I guess there were such guys who were sent over there with special orders, men who were used as special assassins, probably to eliminate enemy officers and such. Harry seems to think that Mr. Long might have been one of those."

Indie's eyebrows went up. "So, he thinks you should be careful?"

"Yeah," Sam said. "He basically said he wants me to keep in close touch with him, and let him know what's going on with this case. I think he's afraid something might happen to his favorite private eye."

"Well, in that case," Indie said, "I definitely want you to do exactly what he asked of you. You're pretty important to me, too, you know."

"Don't worry, baby," Sam said with a smile. "He's got me thinking I definitely want him on my team, on this one." He glanced down at the slip of paper in his hand. "But right now, I think I'll see what Mr. Murdoch has to say about our friend Kenneth Long."

Sam dialed the phone number Indie had written on the piece of paper, and listened while the phone rang. A moment later it was answered by a woman's voice.

"Hi," Sam said. "Would Mr. Murdoch happen to be around?"

"Why, yes, he is," the woman said. "Hold on just a moment, please."

Sam waited a moment, and then a gruff man's voice came on the line. "This is Jim Murdoch," he said. "How can I help you?"

"Mr. Murdoch, my name is Sam Prichard, and I'm a private investigator in Denver, Colorado. I'm calling because I have a question you might be able to help me out with."

"Well, Mr. Prichard," Murdoch said, "how can I be of service, sir?"

"Mr. Murdoch, back in 1969, you served in Vietnam with a man named Kenneth Long. I know that you were captured and held prisoner for a while, and that Long disappeared during that same patrol. I was wondering if you ever heard anything about him again, after you were captured."

There was a long moment of silence on the other end of the line. Sam thought he heard the door closing, and then Murdoch spoke again. "Mr. Prichard, I haven't thought about Ken Long in many years. Can I ask you what in the world has you looking into him?"

"Well, sir, I was hired this morning by his daughter, who had always believed that he died during that patrol. However, according to his brother, Mr. Long has shown up here in Denver in the last few days. He seems to be alive and well, but he claims that he was held prisoner for some time, and was then recruited by the CIA after his release. Is there any possibility that you would have any knowledge of whether there could be any truth to the story?"

Again, there was a hesitation. "Mr. Prichard, I have no idea what might've happened to him after he ran out on us that night. Several of us thought he would be arranging a rescue, but of course that never happened. I spent more than two years locked up in some of the worst conditions that you can ever imagine one man inflicting upon another. I watched several of my buddies die in there. The only one of us who escaped that night was Long. When I was finally released, I found out that he had never been captured, but what really bothered me was that he never even went back and told anyone what happened to us."

"To be honest, Mr. Murdoch, that's part of what's bothering me about this case. There's no evidence Long was ever actually captured; he claims he was held prisoner for a few years and was then released and recruited by the CIA, but he never contacted his family back here in the states. That strikes me as kind of odd, but it also struck me as odd that if he wasn't captured during the patrol, then why didn't he report back to your commanding officer and let Uncle Sam know what happened to you guys?"

"That's exactly my point, Mr. Prichard. Why would he not have done so? Just one moment, sir," Murdoch said, and Sam could hear noises like a door opening and closing. "Forgive me, I just wanted to be sure my wife is not listening. See, she knew Ken back then, and never could understand why he would've abandoned us. I'd just as soon not have her thinking about it again. However, to answer your question, there were things about him that were strange even before that patrol. He would go out occasionally on his own, into the bush. We always thought it was strange that he might be gone two or three days, and no one said anything. If we asked questions, we were told that he was out on a special assignment and to stop asking, and he would never tell us anything. When he got back, sometimes, he would be up at the captain's hut for hours. Debriefing, we figured, from whatever special assignment he'd been out on. The only thing we ever knew for sure was that, after one of his special assignments, some top officer from the other side would no longer be a problem for us."

"So you think he was taking out enemy officers?" Sam asked.

"I think that it's a very distinct possibility," Murdoch said. "I also think that I'd rather not be thinking about this at all. You see, there were other strange things going on around that time. If you know about the patrol, then you know about me and the others who were captured that night. But I'll bet you never heard of Jimmy Simpson."

"Jimmy Simpson? No, I don't know that name. Who is Jimmy Simpson?"

"Private Jimmy Simpson was a new kid. He came in with replacements for some guys we'd lost in an earlier skirmish, and he was about as green as you could get. He was fresh out of AIT, barely even knew which end of his M-16 to hold onto, and which end to point at the enemy. He wasn't even 19 years old yet, and he thought Ken was some sort of super soldier. Jimmy wanted to be just like him. He followed him everywhere, all around our compound, and one night when no one was paying enough attention and we weren't expecting to go out on any missions of our own, he followed him right out on one of those special assignments."

"And? There has to be more to the story than that."

"Oh, there certainly is. As I said, Jimmy followed Ken out into the jungle that night, and when Ken came back without Jimmy, several of us got in his face about it. Jimmy was just a kid, and we weren't going to stand for him being abandoned out there in the jungle. Well, Ken was about as shocked as he could be; he had no idea the kid had followed him. When he found out, he turned around and went straight back out into that jungle without even bothering to go to his debriefing. He was gone for several hours, but sure as the dickens, he came back with Jimmy. The kid was alive, but he was terrified. So scared that for quite a while, we couldn't even get him to talk." Murdoch paused, and Sam heard a cigarette being lit. "Mr. Prichard, you do realize that this is completely off the record, right? That if I'm ever asked under oath about these things, I'll deny that I ever told you anything at all? You do understand that, right?"

"If that's what it takes," Sam said. "I'm only out to find out why Mr. Long disappeared on his family, not to make trouble for you or any of the other survivors. That I promise."

"Good enough, then," Murdoch said. "Well, it took us a couple of days, but we finally got Jimmy to open up to us. He said he followed Ken a few times, just to see just what the special assignments were all about, because he hoped someday to earn the right to some of those assignments himself. Apparently, he was a lot better at following silently than most of us, because he managed to follow Ken for several clicks without being spotted. When he saw Ken hunker down and watch some VC troops ahead of him, Jimmy dug in to watch Ken. As he was telling us about this, he suddenly started crying, and I mean alligator tears just flowing down his face. This kid was terrified, because of what he saw just moments later. He said Ken suddenly leapt forward right into the middle of about two-dozen VC, and began swinging a machete in his right hand while firing an M-16 from his left, until not one of those gooks was left alive. Now, that would've confirmed his opinion of Ken being some kind of special super soldier, but for what happened next. He said Ken took that machete and began slicing an ear off of each body, and stuffing those ears into a bag that he pulled out of a pocket. Well, that was weird enough, but then Jimmy swore he saw Ken drag a VC captain's body into the middle of the clearing, cut that captain's heart out and eat it." Sam heard Murdoch take a deep drag on his cigarette. "And we asked Jimmy why he was crying, and he said it was because when Ken came and found him, he had warned him not to say anything about what he'd seen, if he didn't want to die. Of course, we told Jimmy that Ken was just jungle crazy, that it got to some guys that way and they became pretty strange. We told him nothing would happen to him, and not to worry because none of us would say he told us anything."

Murdoch took another long drag, but didn't say anything more. Sam asked, "Mr. Murdoch? What happened to Jimmy Simpson?"

"Mr. Prichard, I have no idea. You see, sir, when we got up the next morning, Jimmy's hut was empty. There was blood all over the place, but Jimmy was never seen again. The captain told us that a VC Sapper had apparently gotten through the compound fences that night and taken him. Let me tell you, there wasn't a single one of us who was gonna argue the point." Another long drag. "Mr. Prichard, I do believe, sir, that I have said all I care to say on the subject. And I truly would appreciate it if you would make sure my name never comes out of your mouth. At least, not if you speak to Ken Long."

"Don't worry, Mr. Murdoch," Sam said. "I never heard of you, and I've never spoken to you."

Sam ended the call, and turned to look at his wife. "Well, it seems Harry was right," said. "Mr. Long is a very dangerous individual, and apparently was one of the assassin types that Harry was referring to. And if Mr. Murdoch is telling me the truth, he may also be a cold-blooded murderer."

"Sam," Indie said, "I'm beginning to wish we had never taken this case. You want to see what Herman's dug up?"

Sam leaned forward and scooted his chair closer to hers. "Sure, baby," he said. "What's he been up to?"

"Well, you remember that we just sort of turned Herman loose on this guy, right? I had told him to look in some government databases, but when he tried, it actually set off some alarms. Kenneth Long is classified top secret, and just trying to dig into him is enough to set off alarms on several different levels."

27

"Oh, oh," Sam said. "Are we going to need Harry to get us out of trouble?"

She grinned at him and winked. "Oh, come on, baby, you know me better than that! I designed Herman to spot such traps and get out fast, sweeping up after himself as he did so. There isn't much chance anybody has a clue who was behind the momentary breach, so don't get Harry's feathers riled up just yet. The point is, Ken Long is not just a former POW who decided to drop in on mommy. There's something seriously bad about this guy, and frankly, I'm not sure what we've gotten into. But I can tell you I don't like it, not one little bit."

"Yeah, I'm not sure I do either, but at least I'm only working for his daughter. I can't see that being something that's going to upset him too much, and to be honest, I think I'd rather approach him head on than let him find out by accident that we were trying to learn anything about him." He leaned forward and kissed her. "I'm going to go keep an eye on his mother's house for a bit," he said, "and just see if maybe he might pop up. Don't dig too deep; you never know, he might have people telling him if someone tries to track him down."

Indie nodded. "Okay, babe," she said. "You just be careful out there, you got that? You better come home safe to me, or I'll sick Beauregard on you!"

Sam grinned, and made a cross with his fingers. "Let's leave Beauregard out of this," he said. "This strikes me as one of those cases where he's gonna stick his nose in sooner or later, anyway, and I'd just as soon not have to deal with him before it's absolutely necessary." He got up and started toward the door that led into his garage, but a twinge in his bad hip made him stop and lean against the wall. "Ow," he said, and stood there for a moment, then turned and went back to where he had left his cane leaning against the wall by his desk. "Must be gonna rain today," he growled as he turned toward the door again.

Indie tried to suppress the chuckle, but it slipped out anyway, and Sam grinned as he walked into the garage. He got into his Corvette, and pushed the button on the remote to open the garage door so he could back out.

They had gotten the address for Joellyn's grandmother's house from her during the initial interview. Sam knew the neighborhood, so he drove that direction without bothering with GPS. It wasn't a very long drive, and he pulled up in front of a house down the street about twenty minutes later.

One of the most boring aspects of being a private investigator was surveillance, but it was also one of the easiest. Sam had been adept at surveillance even when he was a police officer, so it wasn't a problem for him. All it meant was sitting in the car and watching a suspect's location, or someplace you expected the suspect to appear. It just wasn't a problem, or at least that's what Sam kept telling himself.

Two hours later, he wasn't so sure. There had been

no activity, with no one visiting the house and no one leaving it. He hadn't seen any cars on the street, and in fact, there had been no traffic of any kind. That in itself seemed a little odd. Of course, there was no way that Long could have blocked the street from regular traffic, and if he could, then Sam probably wouldn't be sitting here, either. The lack of traffic was almost certainly just coincidental, but still bothered Sam.

Ironically, it was just at that moment that a vehicle approached the house he was watching. A late-model, nondescript Chevrolet sedan pulled up in front of the house and parked. Sam's attention perked up as he watched to see who might get out of the car.

A moment later, the driver's door opened and a chubby, balding man stepped out of it. He didn't seem to be paying any attention to what was going on around him, but there was an air of awareness about him, as if he could sense the fact that Sam was watching even though he never looked in that direction.

Joellyn had given Sam and Indie a photo of Long when he was a younger man. Sam held it up and took a closer look, and concluded that with the extra weight and lack of hair taken into account, it was Kenneth Long who had gotten out of the car. He made his way to the front door of the house, apparently unconcerned about who might be watching, but again, Sam got the feeling that this man was completely aware of his surroundings.

He knocked on the door, and it was opened only a

moment later. Sam saw a man's face, and figured it was Kenneth's brother, James, who smiled and let him in. There was no sense of awkwardness or unease in either of the men, though Sam recalled Joellyn saying that Jim was shocked at his brother's reappearance. *He must have gotten over it,* Sam thought, *because he sure doesn't look upset now.*

Sam fired up the Corvette and took the next right turn, then the next, and followed that street for a couple of blocks before turning again to come back to the street the house was on. He parked a block away, facing the same direction as Long's car, so that he could follow from a distance when the man finally left.

Then it was time to wait, again, and Sam sat there for more than an hour. The thought of calling Joellyn and telling her that her father was at her grandmother's house crossed his mind, but he wasn't ready to end this case just yet, and frankly, he wasn't sure how Long would react to being cornered by his daughter. If this man was a dangerous as he seemed to be, and as callous, then it was possible that he might even harm his own child. Sam wasn't ready to make a judgment call on that, just yet.

The front door opened, and Long stepped out. He glanced up and down the street before his feet touched the ground outside, and Sam knew without a doubt that he'd been spotted. Still, Long went to his Chevrolet and got into it as if there was nothing amiss, started it up, and drove off down the street at a leisurely pace.

Sam started the Corvette and followed, turning at the corner just as Long had done. The Chevy was almost to the next intersection, still moving at a normal speed, and Sam allowed himself to hang back as they made their way across the city. A mile from where they turned, the Chevy suddenly whipped around a corner to the left, and Sam followed when he got to it.

The Chevy was nowhere in sight. Sam looked for the closest places where it might have turned off again, but there was nothing between that intersection and the next except an alley that had a chain link fence stretched tightly across it, with only inches between its poles and the sides of the buildings that flanked it.

Still, Sam looked up the alley through the wire, but there was nothing there. It was as if Long's car had vanished into thin air. He cruised slowly along the street for a moment, thinking.

The car had been a block ahead of him when it turned onto that street, so it was possible that Long had just floored it and raced ahead to the next intersection. Sam pressed his accelerator and hurried up there, but there were no vehicles in sight, no matter which way he looked. He stared ahead, but he didn't believe the car could've made it to the next intersection in such a short time.

Instinctively, Sam glanced into his rearview mirror and spotted Long's Chevrolet sitting right behind him. The short hairs on the back of his neck stood up, as he wondered how the man had gotten behind him without being seen. Even if he'd raced around the block, he could not have gotten there so quickly. Somehow, Sam had actually passed him right there on the street. It seemed impossible, but the facts are the facts. Long was behind him, and there was no other explanation.

Sam looked at Long's face in the mirror, and saw an ice in his eyes that was unnerving. The man knew Sam was playing stare down with him, and not only did he not blink, but he held eye contact better than anyone had ever done when Sam wanted to pour on the glare. Sam wasn't accustomed to people who could meet him eye to eye, but he wouldn't let that show. He smiled into the mirror and waved at Long, then pulled over and parked on the side of the street.

Long parked his Chevrolet just behind the Corvette. For a long moment, the two men simply sat in their cars and looked at each other in the mirror, but then Sam opened his door and stepped out of the car. He reached back into the open window to grab his cane, then began walking slowly towards Long.

Long pushed the button and lowered the driver's window on his car, looking at Sam without a smile. "Mr. Prichard," Long said. "You're a private investigator, are you not, sir?"

Sam was surprised that Long had identified him so quickly, but then, he may have spotted Sam's license plate before he even went into the house. "I am," he said, "and I've been retained by your daughter to try to get you to sit down and talk with her."

"I'm sure you're aware that that is unlikely to happen," Long said. "I've already sent word to her to that effect. There are reasons, which I cannot and will not go into now, why I don't want to have any contact with my family."

"But that isn't quite true, is it?" Sam asked. "After all, you're visiting with your mother and brother, and they're your family, also. Your daughter simply wants to know why you've never been in touch with her all these years. She thought you were dead all this time, and finding out that you're alive has been a shock."

"I'm sure it must've been," Long said. "I can't say I'm not sorry about that, or that I'm not sorry that I haven't known my daughter. On the other hand, it's been over 45 years, so I can't really see that there is much hope of making up for all that time now. If she wants closure, then she should have me declared dead. I don't think there will be any opposition from the Department of the Army."

Sam let out a sigh and leaned down closer to Long's face, resting his arm on the roof of the car. "Come on, man," Sam said, "can you really imagine that there could be any closure when she knows for a fact that you're actually alive? All she wants is to sit with you for a couple of hours and have you explain the reasons why you never came home. From what your brother has said to her, there must be something you can say along that line. Can't you give her the courtesy of looking her in the eye while you say it?"

"Mr. Prichard," Long said, "it took me one phone call to find out who you are, and learn that you have been highly instrumental in handling some, shall we say, sensitive matters for certain government employees. I know who those employees are, and generally the types of things you've done for them. That tells me that you probably know more about me than you're letting on right now, so I want you to consider the possibility that giving her that courtesy is literally beyond anything I can do. I'm certain there are things you have done in the past few months that you've been cautioned not to ever speak about; my very existence is classified deeper than any clearance you could possibly have. So let's quit dancing around this issue, and get it through your thick head, and then hers, that I'm dead. Regardless of the fact that I've been seen alive, I assure you that Uncle Sam would much rather have it that way."

Sam stood up again. "I can relay that message," he said, "but we both know it won't satisfy her. How about this? What if I could get her to settle for a phone call? Would you go along with that?"

Long let the ghost of a smile cross his face for a second, and shook his head as if in disbelief at Sam's tenacity. "You can tell her that all I would agree to is 15 minutes on a phone call." He took a pen and piece of paper from the seat beside him, scribbled a number on the paper and handed it to Sam. "Tell her to call this number at exactly 6 PM this evening. Tell her 15 minutes, and that's all. She needs to have her questions ready before I answer the phone."

Long started his car, put it in reverse, backed up and then whipped it out and around where Sam was still standing. Before Sam could get back to the Corvette, he was gone. Sam hobbled back to his car, got in and drove off towards home.

3

Sam pulled into his driveway a half hour later, and didn't bother to put the Corvette into the garage. He had a feeling he'd be needing it again before the day was over, so he just left it parked in the drive next to the Honda Ridgeline that was their family vehicle, then got out and headed toward the front door.

Sam had bought the house more than ten years earlier, when he was married to his first wife, Jeanie. She had loved it at first, and talked about how the three bedrooms upstairs would eventually be filled with the children they would have, but the more Sam got into working extra shifts, the more she got into finding ways to occupy her excess of free time. The end result had been a new boyfriend, a surprisingly peaceful divorce, and Sam with the house to himself. Except for a very short period when his mother had needed a place to stay, he'd lived alone in it until Indie and Kenzie had come along.

Sam had been a cop, and a very good one. He made his way through every division until he ended up in vice, and that's where he felt he'd found his true calling. He'd seen the damage drugs could do to people in their lives, destroying families, literally ruining the lives of both children and adults. Bringing drug dealers and drug manufacturers to justice had given him a great deal of satisfaction.

But then, one day, on what should've been a routine takedown of a drug distribution operation, Sam had been shot three times. All three bullets had been deflected by his Kevlar vest, but unfortunately, they were deflected downward into the joint of his right hip. When he'd awakened in the hospital, he'd been informed that his days as a policeman were over, and he had slowly resigned himself to simply being Sam, the ex-cop.

As frustrating as it was to give up a career, Sam had learned to deal with it. He had adapted, allowing himself to get to know his neighbors and become part of their local neighborhood swap. Besides being a police officer, Sam had the skills of a master mechanic; since a bad hip didn't hinder him from doing tune-ups or brake jobs, he often found himself working on neighbors' vehicles in exchange for help with other things, like plumbing and wiring in his house. The arrangement was a great one, and it led him to some terrific friendships.

However, helping neighbors can sometimes turn into something bigger than you ever expected. When a lady who lived nearby had a granddaughter who turned up missing, Sam's former policeman status led her to ask for his help. Before he realized what he was getting into, Sam had blundered into the field of private investigation.

One of the peculiarities of the case was that the little girl's father was a drug dealer who worked his deals through the Internet. Sam, being only moderately computer literate, had decided that he could use the help of a hacker. He had placed an ad in search of one, using a code phrase he'd learned from some of his former arrests. When a beautiful young woman had answered his ad by literally tracking him down as he ate dinner at a fast food restaurant, he learned that she was homeless, along with her four-year-old daughter. He had proposed a simple trade, giving her and her daughter rooms in his house while she worked with him on the missing child case.

That young woman was Indie, and once she was sure there were no unwelcome strings attached to the offer, she had accepted. Sam had given her money to buy groceries, and to show her appreciation she had made a nice dinner for the three of them and cleaned his house better than it had been cleaned in a long time. Sam had told her he had a lady who came by once a week to clean up, but hadn't mentioned that that lady was his mother, and Indie had suggested that he hire a new housekeeper. Sam took her advice, and offered her the job, on top of what he had promised to pay for helping him crack the drug dealers' website.

Indie was overwhelmed at the prospect of the job

that not only paid well, but provided her and her daughter a place to live. She had desperately been seeking a way to get back on her feet, and this seemed like a godsend. She accepted the offer, which made all of them happy. Indie was delighted to have a home for herself and her daughter, Kenzie; Kenzie was delighted because she thought Sam was a great guy; and Sam was delighted because he enjoyed both of their company and because he loved looking at Indie. Looking at her made her feel a bit self-conscious, so he usually only did it when she wasn't paying attention.

Within days, Kenzie was making hints about Sam becoming her new daddy. Her father had died in a military training accident before she was born, so she'd never had a father figure. Indie thought Sam would definitely be an acceptable candidate, but she didn't think that the prospect would interest him, so she began to think about ways to make the idea appealing.

Sam was way ahead of her. By the time she'd been with him a week, he knew he was falling in love, but just didn't know how to say so. The prospect of another long-term relationship was frightening, and yet the thought of her getting away, especially taking Kenzie with her, was more terrifying than anything else he had ever been through in his life. He decided that he simply couldn't let that happen, and so he bought a ring, waited for the perfect opportunity, and proposed. Indie had accepted, Kenzie had approved, and life had gotten better.

Somewhere along the line, Sam had found out that

he was a pretty good private investigator. He had found the missing little girl, which had involved blundering into matters of national security and led to a working relationship with an old secret agent named Harry Winslow. He had also stumbled into the position of lead singer for a local rock band turned country band, and their performances were quite popular in the surrounding area.

Sam enjoyed performing, especially since he was a very good songwriter, and actually wrote most of the songs the band performed. He'd been a singer in high school and college, but never really thought of tackling any of it professionally; lately, however, the idea had begun to appeal to him.

In the past two months, Sam had been shot and nearly killed on more than one occasion, and on his last case, Indie had been shot. Sam thought she was dead at first, and the thought of anything happening to her scared him to death. Fortunately, the bullet had only grazed her head, but the fact that head wounds bleed a lot made it look much worse than it was. Nevertheless, it had been very terrifying to Sam. As a result, he had seriously been considering leaving the private eye business and going into the music full time. He just hadn't figured out how to bring up the subject to Indie.

It wasn't even that he thought she would object. His hesitation was founded in the fact that he didn't want her to think that he was afraid. The truth, however, was that the thought of anything happening to her, to Kenzie, or to anyone else he loved was more than he could bear. In the short time since he'd gotten his PI license, he'd gone up against terrorists, madmen and a serial killer; now, it looked like he was dealing with a genuine government assassin. How crazy could one man's life actually get?

Sam brought his reverie to an end as he entered the front door. Something smelled good, and he called out for his wife.

"Indie?" Sam called. "Where are you, baby?"

Indie stuck her head through the door from the kitchen, so that he could see her through the dining room. "I'm in here, honey," she said. "I'm making a late lunch, you want some?"

"Boy, do I ever! I swear, nothing makes me hungrier than sitting in the car waiting for something to happen."

Indie laughed. "And? Did anything happen?"

Sam sighed. "It did," he said. "Mr. Long decided that we needed a little face to face, so when I tried to follow him, he pulled a fast one and got behind me. I pulled over and he was good enough to talk with me, but he insists that he does not want to meet with Joellyn. He says the best he can do is a phone call, and gave me a number for her to call later this evening. I'm guessing that if she doesn't call then, she'll never get to talk to him."

Indie's eyebrows went up. "Did you call her yet?"

"No, not yet," Sam said. "I actually wanted to wait until I got back home with you before I did."

Indie shrugged. "Okay," she said, "want me to get her on the phone?"

Sam nodded. "Yeah, go ahead," he said. "Might as well get it over with."

Indie walked out to their office for a moment, and came back with a scribbled note in her hand. She picked up the house phone and dialed the number she had copied from Joellyn's file. "Joellyn? This is Indie Prichard. Sam wanted to talk to you for a moment." She handed Sam, the receiver.

"Joellyn? It's Sam. Listen, I actually got to speak to your father for a few moments today..."

"Oh my God," Joellyn said through the phone. "Oh my God, then it's really him?"

"Yes, it's really him," Sam said. "The thing is, he says there are reasons why he cannot meet with you. The best I could get him to agree to is a phone conversation this evening at 6 PM. I have a number for you to call, and he says to call at exactly 6 if you want to talk to him."

"Why, that arrogant bastard!" she said. "After running out on my mom and me, you'd think he would at least have the decency to be willing to look me in the eye as he explains to me why he did it! Wouldn't you think?"

"Would I think so? Yes, I admit I would. Unfortunately, it's not up to me or you. The ball is in his court, and if this is all he's willing to give you, there's nothing you or I can do about it. I'll be happy to give you the number, if you want it."

"Okay, fine," she said with a loud sigh. "I'll call him, but I'd still like you to find out where he's staying. I want to look him in the eye and ask questions, and he's not getting out of it this easily."

Sam gave her the number, and she repeated it back to be sure she had it right. "Yeah, that's it," Sam said. "Good luck."

"He's the one who's going to need luck," she said, "whenever I get my hands on him!"

She hung up without another word, and Sam set the phone down. He looked at Indie. "Sure would be nice," he said, "to make the client happy once in a while. Have you noticed that most of our clients end up dissatisfied or unhappy for one reason or another?"

"Oh, I don't know," Indie said. "At least a few of them have been happy. I mean, the band was happy when you found out what happened to Barry, and I think Jimmy Smith was fairly happy that he didn't go down for murder, even though his wife turned out to be the killer."

Sam gave a lopsided smile. "I guess you could be right," he said. "Maybe I should just give it more time, or look at it differently." He put an arm around her and pulled her close, kissing her gently and then looking into her eyes. "So, what was that you said about lunch?"

"I said I was about to make me some, and invited you to join me. Don't get excited, though, we're only talking Ramen noodles, here. Would you rather have beef or chicken?"

"I'll take the chicken," Sam said. "What time does Kenzie get home?"

"School gets out at three fifteen," she said, "and I have to be there at least 10 minutes before that if I want to get a decent spot in line. Because of safety concerns, they only let a few cars in at a time to pick up kids. I need to be parked in the line so that she doesn't have to stand outside and wait too long before I get there to get her. Wanna go with me to pick her up?"

"Sure, baby," Sam said. "I'd like that."

The microwave oven beeped, and Indie set a bowl of Ramen noodle soup on the table in front of Sam. She handed him a fork and a bottle of root beer from the refrigerator while her own bowl of soup was heating up. Sam waited for her to get hers before he started eating.

"So, how do you think Kenzie's first day of school is going?"

Indie smiled. "By now, she probably has at least one teacher ready to pull her own hair out, and I'm sure she's made at least a dozen new friends. Hopefully some of them will be in the neighborhood, or not too far away, so that she can go and visit them or have them over from time to time. I know she likes the Mitchell twins, but I think she needs more of a social circle than she's got."

Sam grinned. Jim and Anita Mitchell's twins were around Kenzie's age, and they enjoyed having her over. There was supposed to be an arrangement whereby Kenzie would spend a night or two at the Mitchell's house, and then the twins would come to the Prichard home. For some reason, though, it had all been pretty one-sided so far, with Kenzie spending quite a few nights at their house. Sam and Indie had met the twins, and they were pretty well-behaved children, so they were looking forward to actually having them spend the night with Kenzie instead of the other way around.

"Well, she's meeting some kids at church, now," Sam said. They had recently begun attending services at a local church that had been involved in Sam's most recent case. In fact, it was the very church where Indie had been shot. In spite of that horrible fact, all three members of the Prichard family had liked the church, and had decided they wanted to go back. Sam had been impressed by the pastor who had been the target of a serial killer but refused to hide behind police protection. "Frankly, I think she's more likely to make good friends at church than at school, but you just never know."

Indie laughed, but she was nodding. "You may have a good point, there," she said. "At least, at church, we have reason to believe the parents are trying to raise their children properly, and teach them some decent morals. In schools, nowadays, you just don't know what kind of family the kids might be coming from. I don't think there's anything that scares me more than when I hear about all the school shootings, and then I think about Kenzie being in one of those schools. It almost makes you want to move to some small, tiny little town, but that doesn't seem to be the answer. They've had school shootings even in some of those places."

"That's very true," Sam said. "Baby, if I could think of someplace to move this family to where I knew you and Kenzie would always be safe, we'd be packing already. This house wouldn't mean anything to me, the Corvette wouldn't mean anything, and anything else that stood between us and that safe place would get tossed aside without a moment's thought. The trouble is, there isn't any such place, or at least I can't imagine where to find it. The best I can do is make every effort I can to keep us safe right here where we are. And that's exactly what I intend to do."

"Sweetheart," Indie said, "I know. Believe me, there is no one on earth I trust more than I trust you. Sam, you proved yourself to me even before I fell in love with you. I know you would do anything it takes to keep us safe, no matter what it cost you. That's just one of the many things I love about you, babe."

Sam felt his face grew warm, and knew that he was blushing a bit under his wife's praise. "Thank you, baby," he said. "My goodness, but this soup is good! Did you do something special with the recipe?"

Indie burst out laughing. "You dope!" she said. "There is absolutely nothing you can do with the recipe for Ramen noodle soup!"

"Oh, but my dear, I so beg to differ!" Sam said. "I realize that you have never been a bachelor, but trust me when I say that the addition of some chili powder or just about any other spices can turn plain old Ramen noodle soup into a delicacy fit for a single king! Why, I'm quite sure that if it had been available, Elvis would have happily eaten Ramen noodle soup with hot sauce or Cajun seasoning. I shall have to prove my point to you one of these days, and prepare you a bachelor's feast, just so that you can see how creative a single man can be."

Indie got up and walked around the table to put her arms around her husband. She looked into his eyes, then leaned down and kissed him on the lips. "Mr. Prichard," she said, "have I mentioned today how much I love you?"

"Only once," Sam said. "I actually think that I'm ahead of you today, I think I've said it three times already. That means you owe me a couple more, but I'll take a few extras just so that you can get a head start on me for tomorrow."

"I love you, I love you, I love you," Indie said, punctuating each with a kiss on his cheek. "There," she said, "I think that puts me ahead by one. If you catch up, then I'll just have to add a few more. Can't let you get ahead of me, now can I?"

"Nope, uh-uh, no way," Sam said. "I love you, I love you, I love you, I love you, I love you! There, that puts me at least four ahead. When you catch up with me, then we'll work on the next batch."

They were interrupted by the ringing of Sam's phone, and he pulled it out to see that it was Harry calling. Indie sat down in his lap as he answered the phone.

"Hey, Harry," Sam said. "What's up?"

"Sam, boy, I've just received a call from an old pal at Army intelligence in DC. It seems that somebody, a certain person whose name should not be mentioned aloud over a phone, has been checking you out. Have you managed to stumble into that person?"

"Actually, yes, I did," Sam said. "I spotted him at the location he's been visiting, and while I was tailing him away from there, he spotted me. We spoke, and I told him about my client and what she wanted, but he has declined to meet with her. Instead, he gave me a number to have her call him. Said that was the best he could do. Why?"

"Because it turns out that individual has gone rogue. Do you have any idea what that means?"

Sam's eyebrows rose a half inch. "If it means what I think it does, it means he's no longer in the employ of our mutual uncle. Would that be close to correct?"

"Son, he's not only no longer in the employ of, he's listed as number three on the international most-wanted list! There's only a couple above him on that list, and both of them used to hang out with a fellow named bin Laden!"

"Wait a minute, wait a minute," Sam said. "If he's gone rogue, then how is he checking me out?"

"Well, now, that's a bit of a story. You see, it seems that our rogue had a friend in Army intelligence. He has kept that friendship alive, for what he does not know is that his friend was already under suspicion for other things. As a result, all of his communications are monitored. Your boy called him up a bit ago, wanting information about a certain Sam Prichard, who was parked outside his mama's house. The people doing the monitoring saw the flag that came up when your name was run through the computers and decided that they should report upstairs. The fellow upstairs happen to be an old friend of mine, and when he realized that you are one of my assets, he decided to give me a call."

Sam was shaking his head. "Okay, Harry," Sam said, "now that we've gotten through that, would you care to translate it all to plain English? Remember, you're talking to a gumshoe here. Us private eyes aren't always the brightest bulbs in the pack."

"Translation to English: Long has gone into the private sector, hiring his services out to the highest bidder. He's not only not supposed to be here in Denver, he's not even supposed to be in this whole country. He was dropped off American rosters more than 10 years ago, when it was discovered that he was hiring himself out to people who wanted other people dead for their own personal reasons. In fact, there's a bounty on his head that's higher than my operating budget for a year! Most likely, the only reason he didn't kill you on sight is because he's just a little worried about what would happen when I found out about it. So far, he hasn't managed to get the US of A to expend a lot of resources to bring him down, but taking out one of our fair-haired boys would be a way to get us interested in doing just that. He's a row, but he's not a total idiot."

"Harry, what do you want me to do?"

"Do? Sam, boy, I want you to stay as far away from that son of a bitch as you possibly can! God only knows when I'm going to need you to save my bacon again; I want to make sure you're whole and healthy when I do! Do you understand me, boy?"

"Harry? Is there any effort going on to bring him in?"

"Not at this moment, no. I've been told to leave it be, at least for now. As long as nobody gets hurt while he's in town, we're prepared to look the other way and let him slip out just as unnoticed as he came in."

Sam thought for a long moment about what he had just heard, while one eye watched Indie's face. "Harry?"

There was a sigh on the other end of the phone line. "Yes, Sam?"

"Just how much is your operating budget, anyway?"

"In this dinky little office? Just a little over a million. Tell me you're not going to try to collect that reward, Sam. Please tell me that."

"Oh, my goodness, Harry," Sam said. "What kind of an idiot do you think I am? You surely don't think I'd try to take down a professional like this all on my own, do you?"

"Now, Sam, you listen to me and you listen good!

Long is not the kind of man you've ever dealt with before. Yes, I'll grant you've been up against some good ones, but you've never dealt with anything like this guy. He's not even one that I'd want to mess with, and that's usually a line that gets said about me, not by me! I want you to give me your word you're going to stay as far away from him as you possibly can, Sam, and I want that word right now!"

Indie's eyes were wide and frightened, and boring into Sam's own. If anything helped him make the decision, that was it. "Fine, Harry," Sam said. "I'll stay away from him, you have my word."

Both Harry and Indie breathed a sigh of relief at the same time. Harry said, "Don't go back on that, Sam. I need you, boy; I need you alive and well. Don't you forget that."

Sam caressed his wife's back and gave her a wink and a smile. "I won't forget, Harry," he said. He grinned as the line went dead, just as it always did when Harry was done saying whatever he wanted to say.

"So what was that really all about?" Indie asked.

Sam sighed. "Seems that Mr. Long is no longer the government agent he used to be. He's been fired, and is now considered a rogue assassin."

Indie's eyes went wide. "Oh dear God, Sam," she said. "How do we get mixed up with these people all the time? How on earth can so many crazy things happen to one private eye?"

"Well," Sam said, "if this was a detective novel, I'd say that the author has an incredibly cruel and sadistic imagination. Unfortunately, since this is our lives, I'd have to say that I just have really, really bad luck when it comes to clients." He patted Indie on the bottom, and she got up off of his lap.

Sam glanced at the clock on the wall, and saw that it was almost three. Kenzie would be getting out of school soon, and he was looking forward to hearing about her first day. He nudged Indie and nodded toward the clock, and she grinned. "Yeah," she said, "we better get going."

They headed out the door and got into the Ridgeline, with Indie behind the wheel. She started up and backed out of the driveway, then turned in the direction of the school. It was about ten minutes away, but as she had explained to Sam earlier, it was best to get there early to get a good parking spot in the pickup line.

They pulled up in the line of parents, and Indie complained that they should've come a few minutes earlier. "Look," she said. "There's probably fifty cars ahead of us, which means that Kenzie will be standing outside for a good ten minutes before we get there to pick her up."

Sam looked out the windows and then turned to look at his wife again. "Well, it's a nice day," he said. "I can remember standing outside a lot longer than ten minutes, waiting for a ride after school. Good grief, sometimes it seemed like it took my mom an hour to get there to pick me up."

"That was a different world, Sam," Indie said. "Today, some areas consider it child abuse if the parent isn't there waiting as soon as the kid comes out of the school."

"Oh, good grief," Sam said, "how stupid can they get? What if the parents have to work? What if they have jobs, and live in the real world?"

Indie shrugged her shoulders. "Hey, I'm just telling you the way things are. It's just best if I'm here waiting before she ever comes outside."

Sam shook his head in disbelief. "Okay, okay, I get it. Hey, why don't we just go out for dinner tonight? After all, it's Kenzie's first day at school and I think that calls for a celebration, don't you?"

Indie smiled over at him. "I do indeed," she said. "You know, Kenzie has been wanting to go to that new pizza place, the one with all the games."

"Pizza, it is!" Sam said. "I think I can stand a little pepperoni and some arcade time, myself."

4

Kenzie was delighted to see them pull up, and was even more excited when they told her they were taking her out for a celebration dinner.

"Can we go to Bingo's Pizza?" she asked.

Sam looked at Indie with a look of total shock on his face. "Mommy," he said, "did you let the secret out? How did she know that's where we were going to go tonight? Did you tell her?"

Indie shook her head, her eyes wide and a smile trying to burst out of hiding. "No, Daddy, I didn't say a word. I think she's just so smart that she figured it out all by herself."

"I didn't know," Kenzie said. "I just asked if we could go there because I've been wanting to! Mommy didn't tell me, I promise she didn't! Are we really going there?"

Sam twisted in his seat so that he could look at his daughter. "Yep," he said. "Mommy and I decided that we're so excited about you being in school that we should take you out and have a little private party, just the three of us. And you know what else? I heard they even have go-kart races there! I bet that you and me can beat Mommy in a go-kart race, what do you think?"

Kenzie laughed with delight, but shook her head. "No! No, me and Mommy against you!"

Indie looked at her daughter in the rearview mirror, and yelled, "Yay! Us girls gotta stick together! We'll show Daddy, won't we, sweetheart?"

The nice thing about a place like Bingo's is that there are plenty of things to do, so even if you get there way too early for dinner, you can still have a good time until you're ready to eat. That's exactly what the Prichard family did. Sam, Indie and Kenzie let themselves have fun, playing arcade games and racing each other in go-karts—they were electric, and could really drift around the curves—and before they knew it, more than two hours had passed and they were all getting pretty hungry. They made their way to the dining area, where there was an endless buffet of different types of pizza and desserts.

It was nearly eight PM by the time they were all tired enough to give it up and go home. Indie let Sam carry Kenzie out and buckled her into her car seat, but then she gave him the keys and let him drive home. It wasn't a terribly long drive, since Denver simply isn't that large of a city, and they got home before nine. Indie carried her daughter inside and up the stairs, while Sam got her backpack and followed. He didn't always go upstairs for the tucking-in ceremony, but this time he decided to. Once they had the little girl in bed and off to sleep, they made their way back down the stairs and into their own bedroom.

Sam rolled out of bed the next morning in time to join Indie and Kenzie for breakfast. They had a good time together, and then it was time for Kenzie to head off to school again. Sam rode along as Indie drove her to school, and they were back home well before eight AM.

"So, did Herman come up with anything on our guy?" Sam asked as they got back into the house.

Indie shrugged. "After you left, yesterday," she said, "I came inside and did some housecleaning, and I had just gotten done when you showed up. That's why I was making a late lunch. Let's go see what he found, shall we?"

Sam grinned and got to his feet. "After you," he said. "You know I would follow you anywhere, don't you? There's just something about that wiggle that makes me want to follow you."

Indie glanced back over her shoulder and smiled at him, then stuck out her tongue as she hurried down the hall. Sam hobbled along as quickly as he could, but she was already seated at her desk when he got to their office.

Herman had apparently been busy, because there was a lot of data on the screen. Sam didn't know what it was at first glance, but he was confident that his wife would and that she would explain it to him. This was her world, the world of computers and information; she was his guide to that world, and he had learned to trust her.

"Well," Indie said, "it looks like he's found a few things." She clicked one of the first links on the page and a whole new screen opened up. This one was a reference to the patrol that was lost the night Long disappeared. Indie scanned over it quickly, with Sam looking over her shoulder, then pointed at the comment that had been left by a visitor to the site more than two years before. "Hey, look at this," she said. "Here's someone who claims to have seen Long alive in Pakistan, right around the time when bin Laden was killed. Basically, he's just asking what Long could possibly have been doing there. He wasn't part of any American mission, he certainly wasn't connected to the SEAL team that went in, so why would he even had been in that country? It's a good question."

"It's more than a good question, it's a question that should've been asked in more official settings. Somebody should've been asking questions about this guy for years, now, I think. What else we got?"

"Let's see," Indie said, as she closed that screen and clicked another link. This one opened what looked like a PDF file, apparently some sort of official document that listed various sightings of Long. "Holy cow! Check this out, this guy has been all over the world! And look at the dates, some of these would match up with major events in recent history. Good grief, look how far back these dates go! We got him in Tehran, during the Iran hostage crisis in seventy-nine; he was in Beirut, Lebanon in eighty-three and eighty-four, when car bombings were used on our embassy there, and he's been somewhere close to almost every Islamic terrorist attack since two thousand! Look at this list—here's Calcutta, India, Karachi in Pakistan, Saudi Arabia, Syria, Greece, Yemen, Libya, Egypt—look, he was in Benghazi when the ambassador was killed. Sam, somehow, this man has been close to almost every major foreign terrorist attack in the last 40 years or more!"

Sam whistled, and shook his head. "Baby, there's something really strange going on here. I think it's time to give Harry another call."

He didn't get the chance. His phone rang only a second later, and somehow he didn't even need to look to know that it was Harry calling.

Sam answered the phone by saying, "Harry, how did you know I was about to call you?"

Harry chuckled. "I didn't, but that doesn't surprise me a whole lot. Son," Harry said, "you manage to fall into the biggest buckets of poop that I've ever seen, but somehow you tend to survive them. I'm not sure how you do that, but I hope it's a talent you haven't lost lately. Your connection to this case has stirred up a hornet's nest up in DC that's got people calling me right and left, wanting to know if 'that special man of mine' can bring this person in."

"Oh, Lord, Harry," Sam said, "and what have you been telling them?"

"Why, Sam, I've been saying that I have the best man possible for the job, of course," Harry said. "I mean, you wouldn't want me to lie, would you? Truth be told, I don't know of anyone better suited to this type of job than you, so when my superiors are telling me to have you bring our mutual friend in, I'm telling them that all I can do is call and ask. You don't work for me, I reminded them. Unfortunately, the fact that you're a free agent is something they don't seem to be able to grasp, up there. I'm trying to reeducate them, but I can't seem to find the book called *Reality For Dummies.*"

"That's because there isn't one," Sam said. "Reality is something you have to learn by experience, and even dummies are not immune to that. Good Lord, Harry, what am I supposed to do? I'm sitting here at the moment looking at a list of disguised appearances around the country that just happens to coincide with almost every major terrorist activity for decades! That's what I was calling you about, to let you know that we'd stumbled across this information. Didn't you just spend fifteen minutes a bit ago convincing me to stay as far away from him as I possibly could? "

"Well, Sam, boy, I know, and I guess I may have jumped the gun on that. Somebody bigger than me has decided we need to do something about this guy, and you know damn good and well that you're the only hope we got. Therefore, the first thing were going to do is get your family some protection. We can't let this mess endanger your wife and little girl. After that, you and I can discuss what to do next."

"You know what, Harry?" Sam asked. "I don't know that I want to get in the middle of this. I don't think I want my family in the middle of this. And I sure as the dickens don't want to put them in any danger. I don't know who this guy is, and I really don't care, to be honest. He's not my problem; all I did was hire on to locate him for his daughter. There's no way on God's green earth that I could have possibly anticipated him being involved in whatever the hell it is he's involved in. I think I'm going to bow out of this, and let you figure it out on your own."

"Now, Sam, I can completely understand how you feel," Harry said. "The problem is, we don't know why he's in town, other than to visit his mama, but it seems odd that she's been sick a few times in the past, and he's never bothered to show up. The people upstairs are thinking that there's something more going on than just him having an attack of homesickness. Sam, if he's up to something in his normal line of work, then we probably need to put a stop to it as quickly as possible."

Sam was shaking his head emphatically. "No, Harry, I said no. Good grief, then, don't you remember what we just went through? Indie was wounded, and even Kenzie and our mothers were threatened by a madman with a gun, and from what you tell me, this man makes that one look like Peter Pan! How do you expect me to react? I'm sick and tired of having my family end up in danger, and every time I get mixed up with you, that's where they end up!"

"Now, Sam, that's not entirely true," Harry said, "or at least not as true as you make it sound. Granted, working with me isn't the safest thing you've ever done; on the other hand, look at how much you've accomplished. Sam, son, you are literally the best agent I have ever known, and this is another case of your country calling upon you for help."

Sam looked at Indie, who was staring at him with her eyes wide. She could only hear his side of the conversation, but he was pretty sure she knew the gist of what Harry was saying.

"Okay, first off, Harry, what makes your bosses think that there's any danger in his presence? Maybe the guy really is just here to visit his sick mother, did anyone think of that?"

"As I just said, Sam, she's been sick before. The woman has COPD, for crying out loud, this isn't the first time she's been near death! It is, however, the first time Long has bothered to make an appearance. Now, it would seem a pretty big stretch of the imagination to believe that he's aware she's sick this time, but hasn't been before. Wouldn't you agree with that? That being the case, the speculation in DC is that he was in the country, and probably in this area, for some other reason, and simply took advantage of the opportunity to be close enough to see his mother before she dies."

"Aw, c'mon, Harry," Sam said. "Even if I swallow that, what makes you think there's any reason for me to get involved?"

"Well now, Sam, I can think of one good reason for you to get involved, and that would be the fact that Long has a tendency not to leave a trail behind them. Knowing that you're connected, through me, it's not gonna take him long to decide that you're a loose end he wants to tie up."

Sam rubbed a hand over his face. Somehow, he had already come to that conclusion on his own. Just knowing the type of person Long was pretty well told him that he was already in danger. Of course, that meant his family was also in danger. No matter how he looked at it, Long was becoming his problem.

"Hang on a second, Harry," he said. "Let me try to explain this to Indie." He muted the phone without waiting for permission, and looked at his wife. "Harry's right, baby, this is going to be a mess. Long is bad news, and Harry's bosses are figuring it's kind of odd that he shows up now, even though his mother has been sick and near death before. It sounds like maybe he's got other reasons for being around here, and if that is so, then it could be a serious national security problem. In any event, like Harry says, it's not gonna take him long to decide he doesn't like the fact that I even knew he was here. If he decides to strike out at me, I don't want you and Kenzie anywhere he can reach."

"Sam, let's just get out of town," Indie said. "Let's go grab Kenzie from school and just get out of town. This guy is out of your league, baby, he's a professional killer! Come on, Sam, I can't take a chance of something happening to you!"

Sam sighed. "Babe, the smart move right now is to get you and Kenzie somewhere safe. I'll deal with this however I have to, and once it's over, well—maybe it's time I look at quitting this business after all. Between the money we've saved up and my pension, we can live pretty well, and maybe the music will pay off."

Indie leaned forward and put her face in her hands. "And what if Long is already watching us? For all we know, he could be listening to this conversation right now. Where are we going to go that could be safe?"

"Well, what I'm thinking," Sam said, "is that we'll give Beauregard's two girlfriends a call and have them come get you and Kenzie, and the four of you can go up to that vacation spot you enjoyed a while back." Sam winked at Indie, and she rolled her eyes at him. Beauregard, of course, was the name given to her mother's imaginary spirit guide; both her own mother, Kim, and Sam's mother, Grace, were firm believers in Beauregard, so referring to them as his girlfriends was a simple little code that she understood instantly. The vacation spot was also an easy one to figure out, because it referred to his father's old cabin in the mountains, where they had hidden during the terrorist incident a few weeks back.

"Okay, so that makes some sense, but then what are you going to do? You're still in over your head, baby. This guy is bad news; he's not the kind of lowlife that you've dealt with around here."

Sam grinned. "No," he said, "he's the kind of lowlife I had to deal with the last time you were hiding in that particular vacation spot. I actually think I'm getting to be pretty good at dealing with his type of people."

"Sam!" Indie yelled in his face. "You nearly got yourself killed dealing with that type of people! I'm not sure that inspires a lot of confidence on my part!"

Sam picked up the phone again. "It's what we got to do, baby," he said, before speaking to Harry again. "Okay, Harry?"

"I'm here, Sam," Harry said.

"Okay, first off, I'm getting a pretty strange feeling about this whole situation. Just how sure are you of the people who are wanting us to get involved in this?"

"Sam, my boy, it amazes me how you always manage to ask just the right questions. My big problem with this is that I'm not sure who's behind our involvement. Is it possible were being played like puppets? This is government, Son, of course it is. Does that make it any less our duty to do what we can to eliminate dangers to our country?"

Sam sighed, and shook his head, even though Harry couldn't see him. "No, it doesn't. Have you got anybody we can put on Indie and Kenzie and Beauregard's girlfriends, while they pack up and head out to the vacation location again?"

Harry chuckled. "Sam, I've had people watching all of the above for the last hour, including your mother, who seems to be on a shopping spree," he said. "I'm putting together a team right now and will send my personal car to pick them all up. That's the car they had out there the last time, the one with the built-in Wi-Fi. You just never know when that might come in handy, right?"

"Absolutely," Sam said. "I'll make sure Indie knows that you thought of her. Talk to you soon."

The line went dead instantly, and Sam looked at his wife. "Can you make a phone call through Herman? One that nobody could trace?"

"Yes. It's not actually through Herman, but I think that that's what you're asking me. Let me guess, you want me to call mom and start setting this up?"

Sam nodded. "Yes," he said. "And tell her that I don't want to hear a single word out of that dead Civil War soldier!"

"Even after he saved your life how many times now? You should learn to be grateful, Sam. Don't worry, I'll tell her." She turned to her computer and started tapping keys, and a moment later she slipped a headset over her ears. A dial pad appeared on her screen, and she punched in her mother's cell phone number, then told it to dial through. "Hey, mom?" she said a moment later. "It's me, how are things going?"

Sam could actually hear Kim's voice coming through the headphones, as she said, "I've been sitting here waiting for you to call. Beauregard told me an hour ago that you'd be calling. He also said to tell Sam to remember that things are not always as they appear, and not everyone who's a bad guy is really a bad guy."

Indie glanced at Sam, knowing how loudly her mother had spoken and guessing that he had heard. He rolled his eyes, and she winked and replied. "Yeah, well, that's partly why I'm calling, mom," she said. "We took on a new case this morning, and it's turning into one of those messes that Harry gets involved in. You remember Harry, right? Well, this mess is big enough that Sam and Harry think that you and Grace and Kenzie and I should all go up to the cabin for a little while."

"Yes, yes, I know," Kim said. "When Beauregard told me you'd be calling, he said we'd be going up there. Grace is out picking up groceries now to take along. She should be back in about half an hour, and will be headed your way then."

Sam leaned forward. "Kim, don't bother coming this way," he said. "Harry says he's sending a car with the team to make sure you're safe, all of you. They'll bring you over here, and then you can all go to pick Kenzie up at school and they'll take you up to the cabin."

"Okay," Kim said, "Got it. I'll let Grace know."

Indie smiled. "Okay, mom," she said. "And Sam says to tell Beauregard thank you."

Sam glared at her for a moment, but then he grinned and nodded. As much as he hated to admit it, Beauregard—whether he was a real ghost, or just a figment of Kim's imagination—had a track record of being accurate, and his advice had saved Sam's life more than once, as Indie had said earlier. He wasn't sure what it meant, that not all bad guys are bad guys, but he intended to be sure of what was going on with Long before he made any decisions on how to deal with the situation. If that cryptic clue was a reference to Long, it could mean that this whole thing was some sort of set up, and Sam didn't want any part of such a mess. He did, however, plan to let Harry know what Beauregard had said, since Harry was aware of just how many times that imaginary ghost had been correct.

"You know Kenzie is going to be pretty upset about this," Indie said, after getting off the phone with her mother.

"Why would she be upset?" Sam asked, his eyes wide as he looked at his wife. "If there's one thing she enjoys doing, it's hanging out with her grandmothers. Good grief, they spend more money on her than they do on themselves! She makes out like a bandit every time she gets near them."

"Yeah, well, it won't take her long to realize that her

trip to the cabin means Daddy's got himself in some kind of trouble again. You know she hates it when you put yourself in danger; she's scared to death you're going to get killed! And frankly, her mother feels exactly the same way!"

Sam shook his head. "So we make this an adventure for her," he said. "We don't let on that there's any problem, we simply say that you four girls are going on a camping trip in the mountains while I'm getting some paperwork done. That way, it won't be such a big deal."

Indie looked at him from the corner of her eye, and Sam could tell that she wasn't going to go along with him on this. "She's a child, Sam," Indie said, "but she isn't stupid. One of these days you're going to figure that out, and I hope it comes fairly soon. If you try to tell her that this is just a random camping trip to the cabin, and that you're only doing something simple like paperwork but it's keeping you from coming along, she'll see through you as if you were glass. You're not going to fool her like this, trust me."

"Well, what do you want me to say? 'Gee, honey, Daddy's sorry but there's a crazy man who used to be a soldier and Daddy has to go catch him for Uncle Harry.' You think that'll work? Will that be any better?"

"Of course it won't be better, but at least it would be honest! Sam, you've got to respect her, or she'll lose all respect for you! You've got to talk to her as if you expect her to understand, and then she will. As long as you treat her like a person, she'll accept anything you have to do or say, but if you start trying to pull wool over her eyes, all you're going to do is alienate her. You don't want to lose the bond you've created, Sam, trust me on this. When you lose it, it's almost impossible to get it back."

Sam sank down into his seat and brooded for a moment, but he knew his wife was correct. Kenzie deserved to hear the truth, although it might need to be toned down just a bit. After all, she wasn't quite five years old yet. He was just about to tell Indie she was right when his phone rang again.

A quick glance at the phone told him that it was Joellyn calling. He hit the button to answer. "Hello," he said.

"Mr. Prichard," Joellyn said shakily. "Mr. Prichard, I'm not sure what I've gotten myself mixed up in, but to be perfectly honest with you, at this moment I'm terrified."

Sam put his phone on speaker and motion for Indie to pay attention. "Joellyn? Tell me what's going on."

"Well, I called my father last night like I was supposed to," she said, "and we talked for just a few minutes. Like you said, he told me he couldn't explain why he ran out on us, and I guess I got mad and told him off. That didn't seem to bother him, but when I told him that I had hired a private investigator to track him down so that I could come and confront him face-to-face, he told me that if I were to do that, he would be forced to kill me. Dear God, Mr. Prichard, what kind of man would threaten to kill his own daughter just for wanting to look him in the eye?"

Sam shook his head, looking at Indie. "I'm not sure what to tell you, Joellyn," Sam said. "It seems to me that the smart move would simply be to let him go on his way. To be honest, I have learned that he's not the kind of man you really want to be close to, anyway. At least, that's how I see it."

"Oh, Mr. Prichard, it's not that easy. He called me this morning to tell me to warn you to stay away, something about not paying attention to the people who want you to come after him. He says he knows he'd never get to your family, but that there are other people you wouldn't want him to hurt. Mr. Prichard, he said to tell you that if you come after him, I'll be one of the first to die."

Indie's eyes went wide, and Sam suspected that they were only mirror images of his own. "Joellyn," he said, "I can't imagine that it's anything more than a threat, intended to make me back off. If he calls you again, tell him this—say that I and others are beginning to think there's something fishy about the whole situation, and that I would like to simply talk to him. Tell him I'll be more than happy to settle for a phone call, and that I'm sure he can manage to call me from an untraceable line."

"If he calls me, I'll tell him. Please, Mr. Prichard, don't do anything that will get me hurt. I don't know why he is so determined to keep his secrets, but I know I don't want to be on the receiving end of his anger. I've gotta tell you, I have talked to some coldhearted people in my life, and while that may be my biological father, I hope and pray that there is no part of him in me anywhere. He's got to be the most evil man I have ever spoken to."

Sam made a face that said he wasn't sure whether that was true or not. "You know, Joellyn, someone told me just a little while ago not to always assume the bad guy is who you think it is. Now, I'm not sure what that means, but I'm downright certain it has something to do with your father. Please try to get him that message if he calls you, since I'm fairly certain the number he gave me is probably dead, now."

"Oh, no," she said. "At least, that's the number he keeps calling me from. Maybe if you try, he'll answer. Believe me, I would just as soon never speak to him again, but if he calls me again, I'll give him your message."

The phone went dead, and Sam set it down on the desk. He leaned forward and put his head in his hands, and felt Indie's hand caress his neck and shoulders. "Babe," she said, "you've got to relax a bit. You can't let yourself get all tensed up, not when your life could depend on your reflexes."

Sam looked up at her and smiled. "Baby, this isn't tension, it's preparation. Somehow, I'm being drawn into some weird cat-and-mouse game, and you know how I feel about those! I get the very distinct impression that someone is trying to use me against Long, but I'm not sure there's a valid reason to do so. There's something about this case that just isn't adding up. It's not making any sense, and I think even Harry senses that."

Indie's eyebrows went up in the center, the way they did when she was tackling a problem that didn't make sense logically. "Sam, are you trying to say that someone set Joellyn up to come to you? She's the only reason we're involved in this case at all, but from what she said, she only chose you because of all the press you got over the Unger case. How could that have been a setup?"

"No, I'm not saying that she was set up, or that she's part of the setup itself. What I'm saying is, now that we've been drawn into this mess, somebody has decided that they want something done about Long, and apparently that I'm the one to do it. Indie, baby, I think I'm being set up to kill this man. The only problem with that is that I haven't seen any evidence that he's actually done anything wrong, other than just be a lousy husband and father. Last time I looked, neither of those were capital offenses."

"Sam," Indie asked, "what in the world are you gonna do this time?"

"Same thing I do every time, Babe," he said. "I'm gonna do my best to do whatever's the right thing to do, and live through it at the same time."

5

Harry's driver, George, arrived an hour later with Grace and Kim, and two Homeland Security agents who had been assigned to protect them all. These were new guys that Sam didn't know, but he knew Harry well enough to know that both of them had been checked out over and over before they got near Sam's family. Those two waited outside, while Kim, Grace and George went into the house.

"George," Indie said, "it's great to see you again. How have you been?"

The driver smiled and accepted the hug Indie gave him. Not long ago, he had been assigned to keep an eye on Indie, Kim, Grace and Kenzie, and keep his limo close by so that Indie never lacked for Internet access. The cabin they were staying in at the time, it seemed, was so far off the beaten path that even cell towers couldn't find the spot.

"I've been good, Miss Indie," he said. "I was delighted when Mr. Harry said I'd be seeing you folks again today."

"Don't let him fool you," Grace said. "George is just happy he's going to get to sample Kim's cooking again. He went nuts over her ham and beans last time, remember?"

"Oh, yes, I remember," Indie said, chuckling at George. "But I think he also liked sharing peanut butter and jelly with Kenzie, and watching Disney movies over and over."

"Well, of course I did," George said. "Disney movies are fun, and there ain't nothing like peanut butter and jelly! Especially in good company!"

"Okay, okay," Indie said. "Look, I've got everything packed for me and Kenzie, but I want you all to wait here while Sam and I go to pick her up from school. I think it would be best if she heard this from me and him together, rather than just having it thrust on her as a big surprise with all of us showing up to pick her up. Like I told Sam, she's a child, but she isn't stupid, and she's going to know there's something going on. I think it's best if Sam and I explained to her together."

"Good point," Kim said, and Grace nodded her agreement. Indie had already called ahead to the school to let them know she would be picking Kenzie up early, so she and Sam slipped out to the Ridgeline and drove off toward the school. When they got there, they parked out front and walked inside, because it was necessary to show their ID before the school would let them take their daughter away.

Kenzie was waiting in the school office, with her backpack on the floor in front of her feet. She looked nervous, but held out her arms for Sam to pick her up as soon as he walked into the room. He told her to wait a moment, while he and Indie showed ID and signed her out, then scooped her up into his arms while Indie grabbed the backpack.

The whole thing went better than they expected, and once they had explained to Kenzie that Daddy had to go and help Uncle Harry with another bad man, she simply told him to be sure he didn't get shot again, and to make sure the bad man didn't get to hurt anyone else. Sam gave Indie a rueful grin as he drove them all home.

Another trip to the cabin, Kenzie knew, meant more fun times with her grandmothers, and she was delighted when she found out that her old friend George would be there, as well. She and George had hit it off when she found out that George's favorite movie of all time was Disney's *Mulan.* Then, when it turned out he could make a peanut butter and jelly sandwich, they were friends for life!

Kim and Grace had everything loaded into the car by the time they got back, so after a few minutes of quick reunion and some hugs and kisses for Sam, they were ready to go. Sam held Indie close and whispered his love for her into her ears, and then kissed her goodbye and held the door for her to enter the car. He looked at the two bodyguards, and their nods of acknowledgment told him they knew he was telling them to make sure his family was safe. One final smile at George, and he tapped the roof of the car as they backed out of the driveway and headed off toward the cabin.

Once again, Sam was alone, and it wasn't a feeling he enjoyed. He wandered back into the house and pulled the slip of paper with Long's phone number on it out of his pocket as he did so. He sat down in his recliner, took out his phone, and punched the number in.

"I got your message," Long's voice said. "I'm not sure what I'm supposed to make of it, but I got it."

"Then let me try to put it into clearer terms," Sam said. "Somebody is pulling strings up high to try to get me involved in bringing you in. My contacts aren't sure who's pulling those strings, and that makes them and me uncomfortable. Now, we'll add in the fact that someone who has never steered me wrong has advised me not to consider you a bad guy until I'm absolutely certain that you are, and frankly, I'm just about as confused as hell. Is any of this making any sense to you?"

"It could be," Long said. "The few people I can still trust don't know much about you, Prichard. For example, no one knows just what your security clearance really is. Can you tell me, in such a way that I believe it?"

Sam laughed. "I don't even know what it is," he said. "I can tell you that I know what really happened at

Hoover Dam, because I was there, thwarting the attempt to destroy a big part of our country by dumping a suitcase nuke into Lake Mead. Does that tell you anything?"

Long was silent for a moment, and then chuckled. "Tells me you're a man who doesn't quit, I can say that. I heard a few stories about what happened out there. Not bad for an amateur."

"Yeah, okay, so I'm an amateur," Sam said. "Tell me something, Long; just what on earth are you doing here, in Denver? From what I'm hearing, when you show up someplace, somebody usually dies."

"There's a fair amount of truth in that, but it's not always the case. Sometimes, I just go where I'm needed to either make things happen the way they should, or keep them from happening the way they shouldn't."

"Okay. And which is it this time?"

Long hesitated. "I'm no longer popular with the people you know, Prichard, but that's because we don't see eye to eye on some things. Now and then, I show up in the background of something that those people are up to, something I disagree with, and I make sure they don't get away with it. In this particular case, I came here to stop a certain transaction from taking place, and I've already done so. Since I grew up here, and knew my mother was dying, I decided to stop in and see her. It was stupid of me, and led us to this little dance we're doing now, but no one ever said I was smart." He paused for a moment, then went on. "And you? What's got you so involved in me and my little problems?"

"I'm a private eye, who gets drafted now and then to help out the government. I've been doing what I could, and that's what I'm gonna keep doing. Now I've got people saying they want me to try to bring you in, but if I'm reading them correctly, it sounds more like they want you put down like a mad dog. Care to enlighten me as to why that might be?"

Once again, Long was quiet for several seconds, and then he sighed. "You've got these powerful people," he said, "and the only thing they know how to do is be powerful. They are in positions that make them responsible for the welfare of many, but the truth is that the only thing they care about is just how powerful they are, and how much more powerful they can become. Do you play chess, Prichard?"

"Yes," Sam said. "I'm not great, but I play."

"Good, then you'll understand some of the analogies I have to throw at you to make you understand what's going on here. In chess, you got your king and your queen, right? The king is the piece that must be protected, but the queen is the most powerful piece. She can move in any direction, can strike from any distance. She's the most deadly of them all, right?"

"Right, I got that."

"Okay, now assume that your king is compromised. No matter which way he moves, it's check, but the queen is not in a position to strike and save them. What does she do?"

"She's not the only piece who can strike," Sam said. "She sends another piece. A knight, a bishop, maybe even just a pawn, but another piece who can strike to save the king."

"Precisely. Well, among those powerful people, there are those who are kings—they're powerful, but they must be protected at all cost—and those who are queens. A queen is powerful in her own right, but at least some of her power derives from the king. She's got to protect him, no matter what. Still with me?"

"I think so," Sam said. "If I'm reading you correctly, a queen is not necessarily a female. We're talking position, not gender, right?"

"Yes, yes, you're getting it. The queen is anyone whose power derives from someone more powerful than themselves, someone that must be protected at all costs. The king is a bear, tenacious, firmly entrenched in his position; the queen, on the other hand, is a fox. She is sly and cunning, and while she may seem small and beautiful, she can be deadly if she's cornered. She gained her position by knowing how to manipulate everyone around her, and you can bet that everyone she knows is indebted to her. Any of them will do what she asks of them, as long as it doesn't put them in danger. Do you see where her secret lies, now?"

"People owe her favors," Sam said, "and will do what

she wants, but only as long as it doesn't put them at risk, right? Well, then it's simple. All she has to do is let them know that failure to do what she wants is the greatest danger of all. She has to let them know that that's when her pawns will strike, without warning and without hesitation. I'm guessing that that's where you come in; you are a pawn, am I right?"

"Prichard," Long said, "I'm damned glad you're an amateur. Not too many people would've seen that as clearly as you just did, not without a background in politics."

"Yeah, well, if there's one thing being an ex-cop gives you, it's a pretty thorough understanding of internal politics. While you were talking, I just put it into terms I could understand from the Department. I'm pretty sure politics works the same way on every level."

"It most certainly does. Now, since you understand the politics involved, let me try to explain the rest of it. For a lot of years, I served a queen who was loyal to her king. Where she sent me I would go, and what she told me to do, I would do. I've served her since I was a very young man, making my first entry into the world of politics and intrigue, but a few years ago I began to realize that her loyalties might be changing. There were factions within her ranks that were not as loyal to the king as their position suggested they should be, and it became fairly obvious that those factions were manipulating her pawns in order to strengthen themselves, rather than protect and empower the king.

Are you still keeping up?"

"I think so. This queen that you served—I'm thinking she had a very short name? Only three letters?"

"Yep! You got it. Now, keep that in mind, and think about those factions I'm referring to. Why would those factions, who were only part of the total organization, begin trying to strengthen themselves? Why would they take their support away from the king?"

"Well, I would imagine it's because they want the power for themselves. That would make sense, that they would remove support from the king while building up their own power base."

"Ah, ah, ah. Nope, it's not that simple. Think about who the queen is, and then think about who the factions are. We're talking about groups within the CIA who should be supporting the king—the American government—but instead, are building power bases of their own in lending their support to other entities. Some of those entities are within the CIA itself, but some are not. Some of them are parts of foreign powers, other countries who may or may not be our allies. Would you care to speculate on why they would be acting this way?"

Sam shook his head, trying to focus on all the different images that were running around inside it. Long was trying to tell him something, he was sure of it, but he couldn't quite figure out just what it was. "The only thing I can think of is treason. Are you saying that parts of the CIA are actively working against the interests of the

United States of America?"

"*Ding, ding, ding, ding!* Give that man a cigar! Good job, Prichard, you just proved you have a brain. Now, tell me this: assuming you're one of those factions, what are you going to do about a pawn who refuses to support any action of the queen that is treasonous to the king?"

Sam nodded, suddenly beginning to understand where Long was going. "You eliminate that pawn," he said. "Is that what you're trying to tell me? Are they out to eliminate you?"

"Well, you might say it's a mutual desire for elimination. There are those who think their plans will work better if I'm not around, and I think that America will last longer if they're not around. Needless to say, I'm working on my plans and they're working on their own. Normally, this isn't a big issue for me, but apparently I got sloppy by coming to visit mom. On the other hand, who would have guessed that my daughter would hire the one private eye in the whole state of Colorado who has national security connections? Go figure, what are the odds? You learned enough about me and my disappearance to ask questions of your superiors, which sent up red flags all over the intelligence community, and let the people who want me to find out I'm in town. Of course they're going to try to use every asset possible, namely yourself, to get me out of the picture."

"Okay, now wait a minute," Sam said. "If you've honestly got evidence of treason within the CIA, why haven't you come forward with it? Is it some sort of pride thing? You have to take them down or they take you down?"

Long laughed, a deep and hearty laugh. "Oh, my goodness, I needed that! Thank you, Prichard, I haven't laughed like that in years. No, it's got nothing to do with pride. It has to do with the fact that we're dealing with people so deeply entrenched that any evidence I might be able to point to would be destroyed before you can turn your head to look at it. Can I prove what I'm trying to say? No. Do I know it to the very depths of my being? You bet your ass I do! I've seen good men killed to keep their secrets. Hell, I've killed a few of them myself. That was before I understood what was really going on, but now that I do, I'm determined to do all I can to save my country. I'll probably die trying, but that was something I agreed to long ago, to give my life doing all I can to protect and serve my country."

"But if you can prove what you're saying," Sam said, "then maybe I can help you. I do have connections, you know."

"Yes, you do," Long said. "Harry Winslow is a good man, one of the best. I don't know him personally, but I know who he is, and I know you can trust him. Like me, he has stuck his neck out for his country more than once. Unfortunately, there's not a lot he can do to help me in this situation. The people involved are far more powerful than he is, and he isn't even part of the company anymore. HS has its place, but the company looks down on it as if it were a redheaded stepchild. No, I've got to ride this one out on my own."

"Well, where does that leave me? What am I supposed to do about the pressure to bring you in? If you're for real, then what I want to do is let you do your thing, let you do whatever it is you're trying to do to protect my country, too. On the other hand, if you're lying to me, then what I really want to do is break you into a few hundred little pieces. Now, from what I understand, that wouldn't be so easy to do; however, as you pointed out, I'm not a man who gives up easily. So tell me, Mr. Long, where do we go from here?"

There was silence for about ten seconds, and then Long said, "I'll call you back in a bit." The phone went dead.

Sam looked at the phone in his hand, wondering just what it was he was supposed to do. He knew that Harry's people wanted him to bring Long in, which could mean anything from arresting the guy to putting a bullet through his head. If Long was telling the truth, then no matter what Sam did, he'd be helping those who were a threat to the USA.

He wanted to call Harry, but he wasn't sure if that would be a good idea at the moment. It was quite possible that Long had ways of knowing what he was doing, even who he was calling. A call to Harry could set things in motion that should be avoided. It would be better to wait for Long to call him back, and see if there was anything else he could add to help Sam figure out his next move.

He waited. A half hour passed, and Sam began to wonder if he were being played, if Long was using this time to make a getaway. He thought about trying to call the man back, but decided to wait it out. He was playing a hunch, that there was something about Long he could trust. He didn't know why, he didn't know what, but something told him that Long was not the enemy.

The phone rang, and Sam jumped almost out of his chair. He looked at the caller ID and saw that it was Long's number.

"Yeah?"

"Sorry about that," Long said. "You're not the only one they got hunting me down, and it was time to move in order to avoid a trap. Now, where were we?"

Sam smiled into the phone. "We were at the point of trying to figure out why I should believe you, and what I can do to help you if I do. Got any suggestions on either one?"

"Just one that I can think of at the moment," Long said. "Ask yourself this: if I'm lying, why haven't I already come and killed you? We both know I could, and that you can't stop me. Now, there's not really anything you can do to help me, so if I'm not being honest, why are you still alive?"

"That leads to another question, though," Sam shot back. "Why are you even bothering to talk to me at all? I mean, assuming you're telling the truth, and assuming that I can't be of any help to you, what's the point in explaining any of this to me?"

"That is a good question. Maybe I just jumped at the chance to have someone listen, someone who wasn't automatically assuming that I was the enemy. That's not something I get very often. However, the truth is a little less altruistic than that. Just the fact that you have been asked to bring me in tells me that at least someone believes you're capable of it. If you are, then I'm hoping to turn you to my side. I've at least got a chance of living longer that way, wouldn't you think?"

"I'm not planning to try to kill you, Mr. Long. At this point, I don't see any reason to think of you as my enemy, and that's the truth. On the other hand, if what you're telling me is true, then you definitely need all the help you can get. It sounds like you're dealing with some pretty heavy corruption on a grand scale, and I just don't see how in the world you intend to do anything about it on your own. I'd love to help, but you gotta give me something to work with."

"Sam—may I call you Sam? Sam, I wish I knew what to give you. I can give you names, but they would mean nothing to you. Even your friend Harry wouldn't know most of them, and wouldn't have any way to deal with them if he did. Unfortunately, there isn't a lot of true interagency cooperation in DC, so it's highly unlikely that he would have enough clout to do much good."

"You might be surprised," Sam said. "I can tell you that Harry has surprised me and a lot of others at times. He can be a pretty wicked old fellow, when he needs to be."

"Oh, I don't doubt that at all. As I said, I don't know him personally, but I've known his reputation for more than thirty years. Your old friend there has done more wet work than any fictional assassin you would care to name. He's a very dangerous man, make no mistake about it. Even as old as he is, I'm not in any rush to tangle with him. That ought to tell you something."

Sam left. "Well, it just proves you have a brain. I don't know about all the wet work, but I fought side-by-side with him a while back, and there are very few people I would trust more to have at my side in a firefight."

"Hey, you're preaching to the choir; you don't have to sell me on Harry Winslow. As I said, I've known his reputation for a long time. The thing is, that still doesn't mean he can help."

Sam sat forward in his chair, the urgency of the situation beginning to get to him. "Isn't it worth a try? Look, from what you're telling me, we're dealing with a threat to national security. If factions within the CIA are working with foreign powers against the interests of our country, then something definitely has to be done about it. Apparently you have decided to take it upon yourself to see that that something gets done, but you're just one man. So, okay, maybe you're like Rambo, one man who's as tough as an entire platoon of regular soldiers, but even a one-man platoon can't take on an entire battalion. The people you're going up against, who obviously know who you are and what you're capable of, are going to sit back and prepare. They're going to fortify themselves in every way they can, so that no matter what you do you can't reach them."

"You're right, you're absolutely right. They're ready for me, so the only hope I've got is to find a chink in their armor, a loophole I can exploit and use against them. Now, unless you've got some suggestions along that line, I'm beginning to think there's not a lot of point to this conversation. Got anything more to add?"

Sam rubbed his temples. "Look, Ken—I can call you Ken, right? What have you got to lose by talking to Harry? You don't even have to talk to him in person, we can do it over the phone or you can relay through me. Trust me, I know Harry well enough to know that if you're telling it straight, he'll think of a way to help. What have you got to lose?"

Long was quiet again for a few seconds, and then Sam heard him sigh once more. "The only thing I've got to lose is my life," he said, "but that's been on the line longer than you've been alive. Okay, let me give you the basics, and you can approach Harry. If he thinks he can help, then we'll see about a meeting. Deal?"

"Deal," Sam said. "Fill me in."

"Okay, here it is without all the mysterious stuff," Long said. "There are a lot of conspiracy theories out there, you know that, right? Well, not all of them are bogus. One of the reasons that I used Kings and Queens and chess in my earlier analogy was to set the stage for this explanation. There are many different factions in the CIA. Each of them is led by someone who has some sort of powerbase within the organization. Each of those leaders has formed an alliance with someone in our government, someone they expect to rise to the highest levels. Get where I'm going?"

"I think so," Sam said. "These people tie themselves to the coattails of whoever they expect to eventually occupy the White House, right?"

"Bingo. Now, some of them, back in the late eighties, hooked onto a former CIA director named Bush, and that paid off pretty well for them, wouldn't you say? Quite a few of them rose to power in various areas of the government, and some of them are still there. A few others, particularly in the last few years, have chosen other people in the government to support. More than one have thrown their backing behind a senator or congressman, but a few are interested in a certain former First Lady, who later became Secretary of State. She managed to pull off a few amazing feats during her term at the State Department, even though she had a few fiascoes during her tenure as well, and there are some powerful people in other countries that would love to see her in the presidency. Some of those factions have decided that helping her achieve that goal is the best way to make sure they maintain the power they got, and increase it as time goes on. Now, what that boils down to is that those factions will take whatever action they believe is beneficial to her run for the White House, whenever it happens. In short, whatever she wants to happen, in this country or others, they'll do all in their power to bring about."

"But what does that have to do with working against the interests of our country? Okay, I can see where those factions might try to accomplish things that will help put their candidate in that office, but isn't that just politics? How does any of that constitute treason?"

"There you go, now you're thinking! Those simple things don't constitute treason; however, it's quite possible to put together several different actions, none of which on their own cause any real problem, and have a cumulative effect that can cause problems in other countries that will almost invisibly undermine the candidacy of any opposition she might have. And before you go jumping to conclusions, don't assume that she's aware of what's going on behind the scenes to put her in office. You'd be amazed at how many presidents, senators, congressmen, governors, even mayors get elected not because of their own merits or actions, but simply because someone else sees the potential in personal or political gain for themselves in having that candidate win a particular race. The candidate may think that his or her victory is some great mandate from the people to do whatever was promised during the campaign, but the truth is that someone else simply figured, hey, if he wins, then it pays off for me in the long run. It's really that simple, but you'd be amazed how many politicians never understand it."

Sam's mind was reeling with all of the information that was being crammed into it. "So, basically, what you're saying is that this candidate, this former First Lady, may think she's manipulating things to help her win the election, but the truth is that she's just as manipulated as everyone else. Her candidacy means more to these factions than it does to her, am I right?"

"Dead on the money. The truth about politics is that it's like an iceberg. That little bit on top that you can see? That's nothing; the real power, the real impact, is hidden underneath, and there's so much of it that can't be seen that it's essentially an unstoppable force. Now, when you got a candidate—that's the little part on top you can see—who has a highly visible profile but is easily manipulated, then you have a winning formula for some invisible, unstoppable force to come into power behind that candidate. The candidate, once elected, will either play ball with the force behind it or be eliminated. Remember Kennedy? He thought he could wield the power once he had it, but the truth was that it was never his to begin with. It belonged to the force behind him, and when he refused to do what that force wanted, he was eliminated."

"So then, there really is a shadow government? An

organization within the government that pulls the strings on everything else?"

"Well, of course there is! But you're still not seeing all of it. Sam, if things worked the way they were supposed to, the government would consist of those elected officials that the people voted into office, right? Well, in reality, the government is itself nothing but a collection of shadow governments. Those shadow governments change, because what they're made up of is the factions behind the candidates. The more powerful the faction, the higher their candidates, their iceberg tips, will go. But like everything else, factions gain and lose power over time. One faction may be strong enough to take over a large part of the government this year, but two years from now, unless that faction is very cautious in maintaining its position and power, someone else will be ready to tip that iceberg."

"Then what's changing? If this is the way politics works, why are you opposing the system now?"

"Because there's one faction that's been at work for the last ten years or so, and it's thrown its support behind the former First Lady. Understand, this faction doesn't care if she wins the election; even without a win, she'll be positioned right where they want her, in order for them to gain the most power out of her candidacy. Frankly, they don't even care whether she wins the nomination for her party, because the biggest impact she has for them is simply the fact that she's running. Her desire to hold the office of President of the United States is the fuel this faction needs to accomplish his goals. Sam, can you figure out just what those goals might be?"

Sam thought through everything he'd been hearing, trying to find the thread that would tie it all together. Everything he knew about politics, everything that Long had been explaining, all of it was swirling together in his brain and he was trying to make sense of the mixture. Something about the former First Lady running for president was what this faction was using to build its power, but if they didn't care whether she won the election or not, how much power could they gain? But Long had said it wasn't about the election, and certainly not about a victory, but just about her desire to hold the office...

"There's only one thing I can think of," Sam said, "that can make any sense of the things you're telling me. Are you trying to say that there are factions within the CIA that want to see an escalation in Islamic terrorism against the United States?"

"That's exactly what I'm saying, and I'm really surprised you figured it out. Certain conservative Islamic nations do not believe that women are fit to hold office, at least as far as the extremists and jihadists go, and I'm talking about the places where they're the ones in power. Her candidacy for president infuriates some of them, and those factions are manipulating them into stepping up their actual acts of terror. That Hoover Dam thing you dealt with not long ago? I'll bet that if we dug deep enough, the nuclear material in those suitcases passes through the hands of CIA operatives somewhere along the line."

"But, dear God, what's the point? Are they simply out to destroy America?"

"Sam, Sam, if only it were that simple. It's all about globalization, Sam. One world, one government. Do you want to know what is standing in the way of the New World order? It's the one thing that America is most identified with, and the one thing that those jihadists hate as much as they hate Israel. You know what that is, Sam?"

6

Sam's eyes suddenly wide open. "Oh my—it's Christianity. What you're saying is that these factions are out to destroy the Christian religion, which was the very foundation of the United States of America."

"You got it. Take a good look at the last eight years, and you'll see that this same faction has been at work all this time. Trouble is, the current machine is on its way out, and hasn't accomplished the goal. If you look closely, you'll see that there has been a lot of activity that was designed to further the influence of Islam within the United States, even to the point of having fundamental Christians reclassified as a terrorist group. All that has been accomplished by one sitting president, even in the absence of any major terrorist attack. Now don't get me wrong, I'm not a very religious man, but that has nothing to do with the fact that terroristic attacks on Christianity can lead to the destruction of my country. I can either sit back and watch it happen, or I can stand up and fight. Personally I choose to fight."

Sam sat back in his chair and stared straight ahead. "Okay, this is definitely on the mind-boggling side of things. Ken, how in the world are you gonna fight this? Are you talking about assassination? Good, God, man, all you're going to do is get yourself killed!"

Long laughed. "Oh, I do like you, Sam. You've given me more good laughs than I've had in forever, I swear. No, this is one case where assassination is not an effective tool, believe it or not. Even if I could get to the people in the high echelons of these factions, it wouldn't do any good to eliminate them, because someone else would take their places within minutes. No, in this situation, the only real weapon I've got is exposure. If I can expose what's happening, and thereby break down their plans, then I've got a good chance of breaking this particular faction, shattering it, so that it will take it a long time to get back into power. That's what I'm out to do, and that's why they'd love to have you take me out."

"Well, the worst part of this is that everything you're saying is making sense," Sam said. "That makes it hard to justify doing anything to take you in, or shut you down. Listen, I know I'm starting to sound like a broken record, but I seriously believe that going to Harry is the thing we need to do. I'll work with you, I'd be glad to on this, but we need some serious help, and Harry can give it to us."

"Well, like I said, I handed all of this to you so that you could take it to Harry. If he's willing to help, great. I'm not sure about meeting with him, yet, because I'm not sure how far I trust him. As I mentioned before, I know him only by reputation. You've worked with him, but I haven't, so I'll let you deal with him and I'll check in with you later. I'll keep this phone active, so if you need to reach me on it you can. It can't be traced, and there's no GPS in it. Tell Harry that, so he won't waste time trying. I'll call you back in an hour." The line went dead.

Sam sat there for a few moments, all of the incredible facts he just been given swimming in circles around his head. He had never realized just how convoluted and corrupt politics could be, and the education he'd just received was something most people never learn at all. Those who do usually learned over the course of several years, in college or while involved in political campaigns.

Sam opened the contacts on his phone and punched the picture of Elmer Fudd with his thumb.

"Harry?" Sam said when the old man answered. "Are you sitting down?"

"Sam, I'm an old man. I'm almost always sitting down. What have you got?"

"Harry, if Kenneth Long is telling me correctly, and I believe he is, the people who are pulling your chain to try to get me to bring him in are enemies of our country as surely as the terrorists we took down a few weeks back. I've spent the last hour getting an education in politics that I wish I'd never even heard of. Good Lord, I've got images of icebergs rolling around inside my head, but they have nothing to do with the ocean. They're visual aids on how politics really works, and they're giving me a freakin' headache!"

Harry laughed, long and hard. "Sam, boy, politics is the biggest joke that mankind has ever invented. Unfortunately, it's also one of the most dangerous games that can be played, mostly because you never know whom you're truly playing against. I learned that many, many years ago. Now, are you trying to tell me that you believe we should leave him alone?"

"Leave him alone? Harry, if he's right, we need to throw all the support behind him we possibly can! According to him, the people who want him brought in are part of a faction in the CIA that wants to see globalization as soon as possible, and intends to escalate terrorism in our country and possibly others as part of their plan to make that happen."

"And he may well be correct," Harry said. "There are always many such factions, but unless you know who the players are, there's not a lot you can do about them. Does he have names? Can he identify the people and forces behind the threat?"

"I get the impression he knows who he's up against, and I've been trying to get him to come to you. He says there's not anything we can do to help, is he right about that?"

"Are there things we can do? Of course there are. The real problem is a matter of loyalties. It doesn't matter how good or pure your quest might be; if you don't have people on your side who are loyal to both you and your country, and at the same time your opposition has people loyal to its leadership, then there's a good chance you're going to get your butt handed to you."

"Then where do we start? How do I convince this guy that we're out to help him? If this is a genuine threat to America, then we have to act. Where do we start, Harry? Long says it requires exposure, showing them for what they are. Will that really help?"

"It could," Harry said. "Unfortunately, most of the time, exposure only results in starting a new conspiracy theory. God knows, we got plenty of those already, from who killed Kennedy to where was Obama born? Some of them even make sense, but without proof, they're worthless. We don't need more of that. We need something we can use to shut these factions down. Now, if your boy can help with that, then maybe there's something we can do that will actually get somewhere. If not, I don't know what to say. When it comes to terrorists that I can point a finger at, I can issue orders and get something done. Unfortunately, when it comes to shadows in the DC alley, I don't know who to shoot."

"Okay, then what's my next move? Give me some guidance here, Harry. Tell me what to do. From what you've said, officially, Long isn't working for the USA, but whoever he is, I believe he's doing what he thinks is right in trying to protect this country."

Harry didn't say anything for a few seconds. Sam had never heard him speechless before, and was starting to get nervous, but then he spoke. "Sam, if you really believe what this man is saying, then I'll back your play. Talk to him, get me names, at least one good, solid name that I can send up the line. Tell him I need someone I can get dirt on; that's the only way I'm going to make anyone else listen. There are people I know who can shake things up, but I've got to be able to give them something concrete, something visible and provable. Tell him to get me something, and let me start shaking cages from my end."

"I'm supposed to hear from him within an hour or so. I'll let you know what I can get." Just as Sam expected, the line went dead.

Sam got up and made himself a cup of coffee, thankful to Indie for the pot she had set up not long before she left. That made him think of his wife, and he decided he had time to give her a call. He tapped her picture in his contacts, and put the phone to his ear.

"Hey, baby," he said. "Where are you?"

"I'm crammed into the middle seat of this stupid car," she said, "because Kenzie decided she wanted her grandmas to share the big back seat with her. Just so you know, the middle seat is not very comfortable. And we're still on the interstate; in fact, only been on it about fifteen minutes or so. Still about forty-five minutes out to the cabin. How are things going back there?"

"Actually, you can tell old Beauregard that his advice seems to be accurate again. I had a long talk with our new friend, and I'm pretty sure he's not the actual bad guy in this scenario. We're digging deeper, but I think Harry agrees with me on that. If he's telling the truth, then Mr. Long has been fighting to protect our country from some very domestic enemies."

Well, I have another message for you from that old spook," she said. "He says to tell you to keep your eyes open, because you're going to have to know when to jump, and which way. He says it will be a split-second decision that you have to make, and everything you're doing will depend on it."

Sam sighed. "Ask your mother to tell him that if he won't be more clear in his advice, I'd just as soon he not bother to send me any. Half the time I end up more confused after he advises me than I was before. That gets pretty frustrating, y'know? Anyway, I just wanted to hear your voice. I love you, baby. Give Kenzie my love when you get a chance, too."

"I love you, too, babe," Indie said, "and I will. You know she loves you, too. You be careful; make sure you jump the right way. Give me a call later, when you can, and keep me up to date. Let me know if Herman and I can be of any help."

"I will," Sam said. "Bye, baby."

"Bye-bye, babe."

Sam hung up the phone and sipped his coffee, just sitting and waiting for what might happen next. If there was one thing he had learned from all of his adventures, it was that you just never knew what was around the corner.

He looked up at the clock and saw that it wasn't quite eleven, yet, but he was getting hungry. He got up and went to the kitchen, looked into the refrigerator and found some leftover cube steak from a couple nights before. He slapped one between a couple slices of bread, and carried it back to the living room with him. *There's just nothing like a cube steak sandwich,* Sam thought to himself.

He was halfway through the sandwich when he heard his refrigerator open, and the chill went down his spine. He suddenly cursed himself for not having a gun on him at the moment, but it hadn't occurred to him he might need one in his living room. There was no doubt in his mind that it was Long in the kitchen, so he decided to play it cool.

"Cube steaks on the second shelf," he called out, "and the bread is in the bread box. Mustard, ketchup and mayonnaise are in the fridge; help yourself. Coffee cups are in the cabinet over the coffee maker."

"Thanks," came Long's voice in reply. "I'll be right there."

He came into the living room a moment later, sandwich in one hand and coffee on the other. Sam didn't see any sign of a weapon, not even a holster or a bulging pocket. Long sat down on the couch and nodded in Sam's direction.

"So, how did it go with Harry?"

"Harry says we have no reason to doubt you," Sam said. "He also says there are things we can do to help, but he needs a name, someone he can get some sort of dirt on to let the people above him know that this is a real situation. Got anything you can give him?"

Long pursed his lips and looked up at the ceiling as if deep in thought. He took a bite of his sandwich and then nodded. "David Glenn," he said. "David is a messenger, the kind you don't want to have bringing a message to you. He has a tendency to leave a mess behind him, loose ends that should be tied up, but he gets in a hurry and doesn't bother. If Harry can get someone to look closely at his last few trips overseas, he'll find some pretty obvious and glaring connections to some very bad people. Remember a few weeks back, in the news, a few of our embassy people in Libya were in an auto accident; one, a girl, was killed, and three others were injured badly enough to be sent home? David was there, and he used something called a 'line snatch' to damage the brakes on the car. That's what led to the wreck, and Harry should be able to find evidence to back that up."

"What on earth is a line snatch?" Sam asked.

"It's a set of steel hooks with a long wire attached to them. You hang the hooks on the brake lines of a car, and let the wire drag along behind. Sooner or later, one of the wheels will run over that wire, and the hooks will snatch the brake lines loose, spraying brake fluid everywhere. Next time the driver steps on the brake pedal, nothing happens, so the car sails right into an intersection, a tree, a wall, whatever, without slowing down."

"And this David, he used this trick to cause a car wreck? Okay, what was the reason?"

"The girl who was killed was a low-level clerk in the embassy, but she had been making some minor progress towards setting up a new series of peace talks in the Middle East. Because she and the daughter of a Libyan official had become friends, she was able to get the ears of some important people. That allowed her to introduce them to some others, who were then able to use her friendship and connections to bring up the possibility of a new round of negotiations. If she had lived, those talks would probably be starting within a month from now. When she died, though, and the rest of her team suffered serious injuries and were sent home, the whole thing broke down. She had gained their trust, but the people involved are not willing to start over with someone new. Those peace talks may be years away, now."

Sam sat there and stared at his guest for a long moment. "How did you get in here, anyway? I thought I had the house pretty well locked up."

"Oh, you did. Those digital combination locks are excellent, but what most people don't know is that there is always a master combination that can open any of them. How do you think locksmiths are able to get them open without breaking them? I memorized most of the master combinations years ago, and they only update them every five years or so. But don't worry, your average burglar wouldn't have a prayer of getting in."

Sam rolled his eyes. "Gee, thanks, that's such a comforting thought. So, shall I call Harry? Get him on the phone while you're sitting here?"

Long shrugged. "Might as well," he said. "I guess it's either that, or you and I fight to the death. I can't say as that sounds like a lot of fun, so let's talk to Harry."

"Yeah," Sam said, "talking to Harry sounds like more fun to me, too." He tapped Elmer Fudd on the nose, and turned on the speaker function. A moment later, Harry answered.

"Harry, I'm sitting here with Kenneth Long. We've been talking and I told him what you asked for. I'll let him give you the name he brought up."

"Harry," Long said. "I think this is the first time we've ever gotten to talk."

"Indeed, I believe you are correct," Harry replied. "I'm afraid I never even heard of you until now, but to be honest, from what I've read and heard over the last couple of days, I wish I had had you on my team."

Long laughed. "Well, I have definitely heard of you,

and I would've said that I wish I'd had you on my team. It's the fact that I know some of your accomplishments that makes me willing to even discuss this with you today. I thought you had retired fifteen years back. Somehow I missed your transfer to HS, but that may be working in both our favors today. Now, as for the name you need to look at. Try David Glenn. He's a messenger and cleanup man for Grayson Chandler. Do either of those names ring any bells?"

"Oh, yes, I know who both of them are."

"Good, that'll save some time. Chandler is one of the major players in globalization today. He's very good at keeping it under wraps, but anyone, anywhere who wants to build a power base in the New World order will be doing all they can to get on his good side. Now, he won't be easy to reach, but Glenn, on the other hand, tends to be a little sloppy in his work. It shouldn't take much to tie some internal cleanup jobs to him, which will make him a hot potato to Chandler. If we can get our hands on him, there's a good chance we can get him to give up information that would expose some of what Chandler is doing."

"Before we go that far," Harry said, "just what is it that Chandler is doing that you believe is creating a threat to our country?"

"Chandler, and others like him, are working together to bring globalism about. In order to accomplish that, they've got to eliminate its major opposition, which happens to be organized Christianity, and particularly Protestant Christianity. That means he needs to support and strengthen Islam, so he's organizing many different groups that provide funding, weapons and supplies to Islamic militant organizations, and doing all he can to incite them into taking action against the largest stronghold of Christianity, which is the United States. One of the ways he's doing that is by backing a famous female presidential hopeful, since the thought of a female head of state is pretty much unacceptable to those organizations."

Harry didn't say a word for more than a minute, and Sam began to worry. If Harry came back with the wrong thing, Sam could find himself in a fight to the death. Long looked chubby and out of shape, but there was something in the way he moved that said he could handle himself a lot better than Sam could.

"Mr. Long," Harry said, "you have put us all in a very precarious position. There seems to be merit in what you're saying, and I've known about some of Mr. Chandler's activities for a while now. However, as you're fully aware, getting any evidence against people in positions like his is almost impossible. If we could do so, then there is the possibility that we could prevent some future terrorist attacks from ever taking place. We might also help to preserve the sovereignty of our nation, which is certainly to be desired in accordance with the oaths that we have taken to uphold and defend our Constitution against all enemies, whether foreign or domestic. Now, you are sitting there with the best agent I've ever had, and I'm sure you're aware that he isn't even on my payroll. If we throw our support behind you, and fail, not only will you and I go down, but we will take Sam Prichard down with us. He has already saved this country twice, so I know his integrity. I have also come to trust his judgment; he has decided to trust you, and so I'm willing to take the chance that I can trust you, as well. What do you see as our next step, sir?"

Long leaned his head back against the couch and closed his eyes for a moment. Sam watched him, but didn't say anything, and a moment later, the man sat forward again and leaned toward the phone. "First, we need to shake Chandler up a bit. He's not the only one involved, but he's definitely the big fish in this pond. You need to get started on David Glenn, bringing some light onto his most recent activities. If you can just get a few people looking closely at him, that will be enough to start the ball rolling. Once we get that going, we can start working on baiting Chandler into making a mistake."

"What kind of mistake do you have in mind?" Harry asked.

"I'm not sure yet, but it will have to be something big enough to expose him, expose what he's been doing. That's a necessity. Considering that he's wanting me so badly, I'm thinking we might have to use me as bait, lure him into a trap of some sort."

"All right, then," Harry said, "let me see what I can

do. I'm going to suggest that the two of you might want to head towards DC. That's where Chandler is based, so any action we take will have to happen there. How about it, Sam? You up for a road trip?"

Sam grinned. "Hey," he said, "whatever my country needs me to do."

7

They decided to wait until dark, so that not even Sam's neighbors would see them leave together, so by the time they decided to take off, it was nearly eight PM. Long's car was stashed down the alley from Sam's house, and he went to get his clothes and things from it while Sam packed a bag of his own, slipping his Glock and its holster onto his belt, and then they tossed their things into the space behind the seat in the Corvette, climbed in and headed out of the city. Sam called Indie to tell her what was going on.

"So, wait a minute," she said. "You're saying that you and Long are taking the problem to Washington? Then, why am I hiding out here at the cabin? I thought Long was the guy we were hiding from?"

"He was, initially, but things seem to be changing. I've had an education on politics today that would blow your mind, and has certainly blown mine. Turns out there are things I never knew about how the country works, and they're coming home to bite me in the ass, now."

"So where does that leave us, then? Do we go home, or stay in hiding?"

"For right now," Sam said, "I think I want you to stay put at the cabin. This thing is crazy, Babe, and it's likely to get even crazier before it's over. Keep your phone on and I'll keep in touch, but I think I'd rather know you were safe there, at least for now."

Indie sighed into the phone, and Sam could visualize her face as she did so. Her eyes would be half closed, her lips partly open, as she let all the frustration of not getting her own way slide out of her. She never let herself get mad at him over these things, thank goodness. "Fine," she said, and he detected just a hint of a pout in her voice. "But let me know as soon as I can go home, okay? Kenzie just got into school, and I don't like pulling her right back out like this."

"You got it, babe. Just take care of yourselves, okay?"

"Yeah, and you do the same. And tell Long that if anything happens to you, he isn't bad enough to keep me from coming after him."

Sam laughed. "I will," he said, crossing his fingers. "I love you!" He ended the call on that note, before she could find another way to keep him on the line.

"Sounds like you've got a good woman," Long said, and Sam nodded.

"The best," he said. "I don't know what I'd do without her, now. She and our daughter are what make life worth living."

Long looked at him for a moment, just watching Sam drive. "I didn't want to run out on my family," he said suddenly. "It wasn't like that, not even a little bit. I wanted to come home, I wanted to be there when my little girl took her first steps, when she started talking, when she started school—it wasn't by choice that I missed all those things, it was to protect them."

Sam glanced over at him. "Someone threatened your family?"

Long nodded. "I wasn't as lucky as you," he said. "I didn't have someone like Harry Winslow to give me direction, or even to give me orders. I had a handler, someone who simply made sure I knew who to kill and when to kill. They sent me into South Vietnam with orders to kill specific targets, VC officers and soldiers who were known to cause problems for us over there. When I objected, it was made very clear to me that I had not just enlisted, I had sold my soul. If I so much as hinted that I didn't want to follow orders, someone explained very clearly to me just what could happen to my wife and child. That's why I don't want to get close to Joellyn now, because if I do, then she becomes something that can be used against me. When you live on this side of the darkness, you can't afford anything that can be used to sway you one way or another."

"So, it's like they say in the spy novels? You can't have any kind of relationship that lasts more than a few hours?"

Long laughed. "More than a couple of hours is probably too long. I gave up even thinking about women long ago, just because if I liked one, she became a liability. That's no way to live."

Sam thought about it. "When I first met your daughter, I wondered what kind of man you could've been, that didn't come home when you could. Of course, I only heard the official story, that you had been captured and then rescued. Now, well, I guess I can understand things a little better. And it's not that I think you need my understanding, I simply wanted to understand it for myself. I don't know how I would have survived, had I been in your shoes. I can't imagine not being able to come home and see my wife and child, just can't imagine it."

Long waggled a hand in the air in front of himself. "No one ever knows what they'll do in a particular situation," he said. "If anyone had ever told me that I would end up like this, back when I was in high school, I would have said they were nuts. I never would have believed that I could be a killer; heck, I rarely even went fishing because I hated killing and cleaning the fish. When I went hunting with my buddies, I was the guy who always missed my shot."

"Then how in the world did you get here? What kind

of training could do this to a man?"

"It wasn't so much training, as survival. When I made it through basic, and was sent off to sniper school because I was a very good shot, it suddenly dawned on me that when I got out of training, there would be people trying to kill me, and the only hope I had of keeping them from it was to kill them first. Once I got that through my thick head, it wasn't all that difficult to think of them as targets rather than as human beings. Just like in basic training, targets fall down when you shoot them. By the time I had racked up a half-dozen kills, it didn't matter to me anymore whether they were targets made of plastic or of flesh."

Sam shook his head as he guided the car onto Interstate 70. "Man, I thought I had it rough when I stumbled into all of this national security stuff. I can't imagine what it must have been like for you. Some of the things we found online—can I ask questions, or would you have to kill me if you answer?"

Long chuckled at that. "There's some things I could tell you that would require me to make sure you couldn't ever repeat them, but I like you, so I won't share those things. Go ahead, but be warned—you may not like the answers."

Sam nodded. "Fair enough," he said, "because you probably won't like the questions. Let's start with the Iran Hostage crisis. According to one file we found, you were somewhere in Tehran when it went down. What were you doing there?"

"I was there as a consultant to Crandall Oil," Long said. "Now, if you understood the world I live in, you'd know that being a consultant means I was there to eliminate certain opposition to Crandall's efforts at securing oil leases they wanted from the de facto Iranian government. Remember that the Shah had been deposed and was gone, and the new government going into place was something of a theocracy, or at least it was planned to be. Some of the so-called officials that were suddenly occupying offices in that government were more interested in personal gain than in serving their country, and wanted ever bigger and better bribes from Crandall. Trouble was, no matter how well or how much the company paid off, the officials wanted more. Someone in the area of the CIA that handled me decided that we needed to give them the idea that cooperation was the way to get what they wanted, and that demanding more money was the way to get dead. It was purely coincidental, but you've heard about the six diplomats who escaped? The ones they snuck out of there as part of a phony film crew? Well, as the students were flooding into the embassy, two different groups walked away, trying to escape. The idea was for them to go to the British Embassy, but they didn't make it. One of them was rounded up by students and forced to go back to the to the US Embassy, but the other almost got through. The trouble was that the British Embassy was also surrounded by protesters, so they couldn't get inside. One of them, Bob Anders, lived not too far away and decided he wanted to take his group to his house, to try to hide there. Well, as I said, it was purely coincidental, but when he decided to detour to his place, I happened to be standing on the corner, and he spotted me. He knew who I was, and why I was there, so he asked me to help them get to his house. I did, and then went on about my own business, and never knew that they were stuck there. They ended up hiding with the Canadian ambassador and some of his staff for almost three months. Of course, by that time, I was long gone."

Sam glanced over at him. "This is weird," he said. "What you're talking about, to me, is history; to you, it's memories, something you lived through. That's amazing to me."

"Yeah, well, that's life."

"You were talking earlier about that former First Lady who became Secretary of State. I noticed that you were also at Benghazi when that Embassy was attacked. Were you connected to that in some way?"

"No, though I think I should've been. I was there on a simple elimination job, taking out a foreign agent who was causing us some troubles. I was in a different part of the city, and the whole thing was over before I even knew what was happening. If I had known, I might have been able to get there and help."

Sam drove in silence for a while, and they passed into Kansas. It wasn't late in the day, and Sam wanted to make time while he could. There wasn't a lot of traffic on their side of the highway, and the Corvette was cruising along beautifully.

"This is a nice car," Long said after a half hour of quiet. "I'll bet you built it yourself?"

"Pretty much," Sam said. "I bought it at a police auction, after it was seized in a drug raid. She'd suffered some damage, and needed a lot of TLC to get her back to top shape. When I got shot and retired from the force, she's what kept me going for a while, there. I needed something to help me focus, y'know, keep me thinking of myself as alive and well. The Vette did the trick."

"She's sweet. Cars are another thing I never got to hold on to. In my life, anything that becomes a habit is something that can be used to track you down, and if it's any kind of addiction, even the way a hobby can be addicting, then it's another liability. Car like this, an enemy might use it as a threat to hold over your head. I can't have anything I'm not prepared to let go of in an instant."

Sam smiled. "I'm glad I don't live in your world," he said. "I like my car, I like her a lot."

"Yeah, I'm sure you do. I'd like her, too, if I could and she was mine."

The silence settled back in, and they rode along without speaking for a couple of hours, then Sam announced a need to stop and stretch his legs. Long nodded, and agreed that he could use a short break himself, so they pulled off at a gas station at the next exit. Sam went into the bathroom, while Long stood out in the store and watched the traffic that came in and out, and then Sam kept watch while Long made himself more comfortable. They each grabbed a snack and a soft drink, then got back into the car and headed out again.

"I haven't been to DC in years," Sam said, "not since I was there in college. Has it changed a lot in the past decade?"

Long looked at him. "You're asking me? Do you think I hang out there? This will be my second trip to that city; the first was when I was called in to meet some people who needed information I happened to have, back in Reagan's day. I didn't leave anything there I cared about, and wouldn't be going there now if it weren't for the need to make sure Chandler and his cronies get what's coming to them."

Sam smiled. "Great. We're on our way to what may be a trap, and neither one of us knows the lay of the land. Sounds like a great setup for success, doesn't it?"

Long shrugged. "One of the things I've learned is that there isn't any formula for success. You either accomplish your mission or you don't, and if you don't, then all you can do is try to get out alive. So far, I've been lucky on that score."

"Got any idea what we should do when we get there? What our first real move should be? Maybe some sort of a hint so I don't walk in and blow whatever it is we're trying to do?"

"Not even a glimmer," Long said. "On the other hand, I suspect we'll know exactly what to do by the time we arrive. Unless your pal Harry is doing something extraordinary in covering for us, there's very little doubt in my mind that the people who want to shut me up are fully aware that we're coming that direction. That being the case, I think our first move will be pretty obvious by the time we get there."

Sam shook his head. "So, if somebody is shooting at us when we get there, then it's pretty obvious we should check back, right? I think I could've figured that one out on my own."

"Yeah, probably," Long said with a laugh. "That one shouldn't be too hard for anybody to figure out, but then, I have known a few who weren't that bright. Maybe someday I can tell you a few stories."

"Nah, I'm good," Sam said. "All I want to do is get through this one, and get back to my family."

It was nearly seven PM by the time they stopped again, to grab a bite to eat and gas up. Sam gave Indie a call as they got back on the road and talked with her for a few minutes, saying goodnight to Kenzie even though he knew they wouldn't get her into bed before ten. When he finished that call, he decided to try Harry again.

"Sam, I do believe we have opened a can of worms,"

the old man said as he answered. "It seems that we are not the only ones paying close attention to Mr. Glenn, and some of the things he's been doing in the last few months. Just by mentioning his name, I have set off a bit of a storm up there, and it seems that Chandler and others are doing all they can to distance themselves from him quickly."

Sam had the phone on speaker, and Long was nodding. Sam said, "Ken, here, doesn't seem surprised. Are you?"

"Not particularly," Harry said, "but things are definitely happening more quickly than I had anticipated. Glenn is out of the country, and there have been orders sent out to have him return immediately. Now, whether he will obey those orders or not remains to be seen. All I'm trying to do is keep an eye on the situation so that I can advise you on who to contact when you arrive."

"And we appreciate it," said Long. "There has to be someone up there who stands to gain by seeing Chandler come down. At the very least, we need someone who can see the big picture and is willing to step up to the plate to help us stop this faction from succeeding in their goals."

"Yes, that's how I see it, too," Harry said. "At the moment, I'm testing all of my contacts and trying to see which of them would be best for you gentlemen. I don't want anyone knowing that the two of you are on this trip until we're actually ready to make a move."

"Good. That's how I want it, also. The more surprise we have on our side, the better our chances of success and survival. Remember, this isn't a strike mission; we're not out to draw blood or kill anyone, we're simply trying to shed light on something that wants to stay hidden in the darkness."

"Yes, we know," Harry said, and Sam agreed. "That's why I want the proper ally for you as soon as you get there. You, Mr. Long, are expendable; you've known that your entire professional life, just as I have. Sam is not, or at least, we want to keep him alive and healthy for as long as we possibly can. And just so you know, that's not entirely because I'm afraid of what his wife would do to me if he got hurt, but I'll confess that it's in there."

Sam laughed. "It'd better be," he said. "I know Indie, and it's definitely one of the things you need to keep in the forefront of your thoughts."

"Yes, I'm sure it is. I'll let you know if I learn anything else, boys, but it's time for this old man to have a bite to eat." The line went dead.

Long looked at Sam. "He's a man of few words, isn't he?"

"Only 'til you get to know him, and then it's hard to get him to shut up. But if Harry says he's got your back, then you can count on him. The first time I met him, he was holding my wife—she was just an employee at the time—as a hostage to get me to keep an appointment to meet with him, but as soon as we got together, he basically let me make him my prisoner so that I'd have reason to listen to the story he wanted to tell me."

"Then, you probably got to hear all about his time with the SEALs and on the Al Qaeda desk, right? Those are true, but don't believe him if he tries to say he wasn't a killer; Harry Winslow has a confirmed kill list that no one has matched since his days in the field."

"Yeah, I know he's been there," Sam said. "All he'll say about it is that he's done what had to be done, and it wasn't always nice, but it isn't hard to read between the lines. Harry's a good man, but he's a hard man, too."

"True. Right now, to be perfectly honest, I'm kind of glad he's willing to go with us on this. With his support, it's possible we can pull it off and manage to keep the USA intact a few years longer."

Sam turned to look at him. "A few years longer? Then you expect globalism to come sooner or later, now matter what we do?"

"It's coming, there's no doubt about that. I'm not going to delude myself into thinking I can stop it, but I'm going to do all I can to delay it. I don't want to see it in my lifetime."

Sam shrugged. "I'm sure none of us do, but if it's inevitable..."

Long looked over at him. "You go to church, Sam?"

"Yeah," Sam said. "We just started, actually, but I've gone to church off and on since I was a kid."

"Did you know that every government on earth studies Bible prophecy? That's because, over the past three thousand years or so, there have literally been hundreds of Biblical Prophecies that have come true, and so clearly have they come true that in some cases, it was possible to see it coming true as it happened. The prophet Daniel, for example, foretold a King of Macedonia that would conquer Persia, and set Jerusalem free from Persian dominion, and when Alexander the Great was shown this prophecy, he was so amazed at how accurately it described him and his kingdom that he went into the Jewish temple and made a sacrifice to the Jewish God, then left Jerusalem undisturbed. He went on to conquer the Persian Empire, just as Daniel had predicted."

Sam stared at him. "So, you're saying that prophecy says globalism is unavoidable?"

"Absolutely," Long said. "So many of those prophecies have come true that every nation has a department that studies it, and particularly the books of Daniel and Revelation. The New World Order is coming, Sam, and all I'm trying to do is slow it down a bit."

Sam shook his head. "What was that you said a while ago, about not being a religious man?"

"Oh, I'm not," Long said. "You don't have to be religious to know that there's something to prophecy. I mean, look at Nostradamus, and all the things he wrote that seem to have predicted everything from Hitler to Apollo Eleven."

Sam looked at him again, and then drove on without speaking anymore for a while.

8

Grayson Chandler was a man who knew his way around Washington, which he should, since he'd been there for more than forty years. At sixty-two years old, he'd gone from an unpaid intern on the staff of Senator Strom Thurmond in nineteen seventy-three to the Senior Islamic Analysis Desk of the CIA, and he had the personal cell numbers of literally hundreds of American and foreign politicians. He knew who to call to get a favor, and there were plenty who knew that he was the one to call if you needed something done quickly.

Chandler often told himself that, despite what most people believed, he was easily the most powerful man in the United States, simply because he knew where so many bodies were buried. He should; he'd buried some of them personally, and many more had been on his orders. When you had that kind of information, you could get anything else you wanted, whether it be other information, money, power or whatever it took to help someone else who had a problem they needed dealt with. He'd dealt with a lot of problems for people in Washington, and for many people in other places around the world.

He had a team of people who handled those problems for him, and it was one of those team members who was on his mind that evening. David Glenn, a man he'd often used the past few years to get things done, had suddenly come under some sort of unexpected scrutiny earlier in the day, and Chandler had to figure out just how to best handle the problem. It wasn't that big a deal, he knew. Luckily, Glenn was out of the country at the moment; if nothing else, he would simply have the man vanish, just as so many others had done when they became liabilities. There was always someone ready and willing to take their places, and it was easy to leave a fake trail showing that an agent had gone rogue. After all, in a world where money was what most people worshiped and prayed for, almost anyone could understand why someone would betray his country for enough of the stuff.

Another email came in, and he glanced at it to confirm that it was on the same topic; someone at Homeland Security, it said, was calling for Glenn to come and answer questions about the accident in Libya, and once the questions began, Chandler knew, they wouldn't stop. Glenn had been around since the Monica Lewinsky scandal, and if Chandler had been told about

Lewinsky only a day sooner, that fiasco could have been contained. Glenn would have done what was necessary, and Monica would have joined a few other girls who suddenly vanished.

Oh, well. He typed up a message to one of his assets in Baghdad, encoded so that only the man it was intended for would know what the message truly said, and sent it off. Glenn would cease to be an issue before the sun rose again.

Now, to find out who in HS was making waves—ah, well, what a surprise. Harry Winslow, eh? And just the day before, he'd sent word through proper channels requesting that Harry's people deal with another problem, namely Kenneth Long. Long was in Harry's yard at the moment, messing up some of Chandler's minor plans and making surreptitious visits to see his sick mother. Chandler didn't have anyone who could get into Denver without leaving a trace that would be hard to explain, but he'd forced Long out into the cold years ago; the man was listed as a rogue, and so he was fair game for anyone who could take him down. One of Harry's superiors said he had a man who could get things done, so Chandler had made the request.

And now Harry was asking questions about Dave? That made it sound like Long was getting to someone on Harry's team, and it was probably that greenie who kept bumbling into NatSec matters. That was going to be an issue, because Harry was rather well entrenched. He could get some serious ears, if he really wanted them, so it behooved Chandler to start working on a way to deal with the questions that were bound to come up.

He picked up his phone and dialed a number from memory. "Oscar?" he said, when it was answered. "Hey, it's Grayson, how you been?"

He could sense the immediate tension in the other man's voice, and it made him smile. Chandler had always liked knowing that people feared him, for fear was just the most basic from of respect.

"I'm doing okay, Grayson," Oscar said nervously. "And you?"

"Not bad, not bad. Listen, I have a little problem, and it occurred to me that you might be the one to help me out with it, are you game?"

"Yeah, sure," Oscar said; no one ever declined to help Chandler with one of his problems, because those who had done so in the past seemed to have their entire worlds crumble around them. "What can I do for you?"

"Well, it shouldn't be too big a deal. What I need is to get a lead on Harry Winslow's man in Denver. His name is Prichard, and I know you've got an asset there, right?"

Oscar Rogo was almost seventy, but his mind was as sharp as ever. He'd been with the IRS for more than forty years, and had gone into private sector consulting when he'd been forced to retire, but he'd built himself a network of people he could trust, and used it to keep track of things that might help him solve problems for his clientele. One of those people, as Chandler said, was in Denver.

"Yeah, I can call Frank Monetti, there. What do you need to know?"

Chandler smiled. "Just ask him to check up on Prichard, see what he's up to at the moment. If he can get an idea of who he might be hanging out with, that could help me out, too. And, Oscar, thanks! This could mean a lot to me, and I'll owe you one."

"Hey, no, you don't owe me anything," Oscar said. Like a lot of others, he didn't want Chandler owing him any favors, because somehow, when he paid up, it turned out that he overpaid and you ended up owing him a lot more. "Glad to help out a friend, no problem! I'll call Frank now, and get back to you as soon as I can."

"Hey, thanks, Oscar, this is really terrific of you! Talk to you soon!"

Chandler ended the call, and sat back in his chair, taking a sip of vodka from the glass he held in his hand. He'd come to love the smooth feel of the liquor as it slid down his throat, and the way it relaxed him without dulling his wits. He couldn't afford to let anything do that to him, he knew, no matter how safe at home he might think he was. There were always enemies waiting or any opportunity to pounce on him, take away all he'd worked for all these years, and he couldn't risk that happening.

So, okay, he'd dealt with Glenn, and by morning he should know what Prichard was doing with Long. If

Long had actually gotten to Harry, that might get a little messy, but it shouldn't be too hard to deal with. After all, Harry was an old man, and there were essentially undetectable drugs that could make an old heart fail suddenly. Who would be surprised if Harry died of heart failure, after all he'd been through over the years?

The wild card in all of this would be Prichard. While he wasn't an actual government agent, he'd been so instrumental in foiling plots against the country that he could probably get someone to listen to him, if he really wanted to. Maybe it was time he found out just who Chandler was, and why it was wise not to cross him. Once he heard from Oscar's man, he'd send someone in to get a little leverage on Prichard. Maybe the guy had a wife or kids; they were always good leverage.

All of that could wait until morning, though. It was getting late, and he'd promised Janice that he'd watch some TV with her that night, so he capped the vodka and drained the last of it from his glass, then rinsed it in the sink on the bar. This was his den, his personal domain, and not even Janice would come into it uninvited. He set the glass to dry and then went to find his wife in the living room.

* * * * *

From Denver to Washington was a drive of almost seventeen hundred miles, and Sam had figured it for about twenty-four hours, not counting stops. At midnight, he'd reluctantly let Long have the keys to the

Corvette, because he was having trouble keeping his eyes open and didn't want to stop. When he woke up, it was almost seven the next morning, and he was feeling pretty well rested.

It struck Sam as odd that, only the morning before, he'd been worried that Long might be a danger to him and his family, but now he was on a cross country journey with the man to try to prevent a traitor from handing over control of America to some global government that was predicted thousands of years before. Sam had grown up in church, something his father had insisted on when he was young, but he'd never gotten deeply into any of the prophecy stuff; hearing that so much of what was happening today, and what had already happened in the past, was predicted in such amazing detail that it could be understood even by a layman was quite a shock to him. If he lived through this, and didn't end up in some federal prison for aiding a rogue agent, he'd start looking into it.

For now, though, all Sam really cared about was figuring out what to do next. If Long was right, then there were people in DC who were actively working against the best interests of the USA, and neither of them was willing to let that continue.

He looked over at Long, who was driving. "Where the heck are we?"

Long grinned. "We'll be hitting Chicago in about twenty minutes. This thing'll really cruise; I've been making some good time."

Sam grinned. "Yeah, she'll get right on down the road. Last time I had her out on the Interstate, I was being chased by people I thought were out to kill me and the man I'd gone to track down. I was pretty glad I hadn't skimped on the engine, then."

"I'd imagine so. Feel like grabbing some breakfast and taking the wheel for a while? I'm starting to get tired, and I could use a bite to eat before I crash."

Sam nodded, and pointed to a sign for a Bob Evans Restaurant that was coming up at the next exit. Long smiled. "Biscuits and gravy, here I come!" he said, and Sam laughed.

The exit appeared on schedule, and they followed the signs to get to the restaurant, then parked the Vette in front of the building and went inside. They both made the restroom their first stop, but Sam was in and out quickly, while Long needed to take a few extra minutes. Sam wandered through the gift shop that was attached to the restaurant, and bought Kenzie a couple of toys, then found a wall plaque that said, "*WIFE stands for Witty, Intelligent, Faithful, Exotic, and don't you forget it, Buster!*" and smiled as he bought it for Indie. Long came out as he was paying for his purchases, and they went in to find a booth.

A waitress brought them coffee and took their orders, then left them to look around the place. The company bought lots of farmhouse-type antiques to use as décor, and Sam got a kick out of seeing so many things he knew only from reading about earlier times. He saw what he thought was a butter churn, and another item he figured must be used for stretching fence wire. Long seemed amused by his curiosity.

"What?" Sam asked. "I suppose you know what all those things on the walls are for?"

Long looked around. "Well, most of them, anyway. Don't you?"

Sam shrugged. "Most of them," he said. "I always sort of wished we'd lived in the country when I was growing up. I think I would've been a great farm kid, y'know?"

Long took a sip of coffee and shook his head. "And I grew up on a farm, hated every second of it, and wanted to live in the city. When my dad died, I was sixteen; Mom and my brother and I all moved into Denver as soon as Mom could sell the farm, because she didn't know how to run it, and my brother and I were too young. A neighbor made an offer, and she took it, and we lived okay for a while."

Sam looked at him. "What made you join the Army? You said you were more the pacifist type, so I'm curious why you'd join up, especially when we were at war in Vietnam."

"Ha!" Long said. "I actually got a choice handed to me—go to the Army, or go to jail for two years. I'd gotten into some minor trouble with some buddies, breaking into some abandoned buildings and such. Well, one of them wasn't completely abandoned, because the company that owned it, a brewery, kept some beer stored there, and we stole some of it. Of course, we got so drunk that we got caught, and the judge gave me that choice. I was already engaged to Maggie, Joellyn's mother, so we got married and a month later I signed up for a four-year hitch. I had no idea I'd turn out to be such a good shot, or that I'd get drafted into this life, but by the time my daughter was born, I knew I'd never be able to go home again. The rest I told you, about how I came to accept it all."

Sam nodded. "Seems to me that you got the shaft," he said. "I mean, you never even got to go home and meet your kid, or be with your family. Why couldn't you have had a secret life, like they show in movies? Have a home life with the family, and go off on missions that are disguised as business trips?"

"You, my friend, have watched too many spy movies made in Hollywood. Most real agents don't get to have families, not if they're going to do their jobs. A family is nothing but a bag of liabilities and limits; they can be used against you as a threat, and the more you worry about anyone ever finding out about them, the less effective you can be. And if you stop being effective, then someone up at the top of the food chain decides that you know too much, and a new young guy, who's just like you were when you began, gets sent to put you down." Long caught the surprise in Sam's eyes. "What? You're shocked that after years of doing what we do, our final reward is going to be a bullet in the head? Guys like me, Sam, we know it all along. The people who pull our strings know that we know where bodies are hidden, and that makes them nervous. When we're no longer useful, or we get old, they have to get rid of us in order to protect themselves."

"Is that why you went rogue? To make it harder for them to track you down and kill you?"

Long grinned at him again. "Let me explain something to you," he said. "I didn't 'go rogue,' not at all. I simply became a liability to someone up high, maybe even Chandler himself. Someone I'd done a job for, somewhere along the line, declared me rogue in order to discredit me. That's why I can't just go to someone with the things I know and expose people like that, I have to find someone I can trust. You and Harry would have been the last ones I would have expected to help me out, but now that you are, I'm not going to waste the opportunity. If we make it, we'll have done something good."

"And if we don't?"

"Well, then, we'll probably be dead, all three of us. I'll be shot down and buried as a John Doe, Harry will die of a heart attack or something similar, and you—you'll be posthumously awarded a medal, probably, maybe for getting yourself killed while saving the world from a madman who looks like me."

Sam shook his head. "You're just the most cheerful and optimistic guy, aren't you? Don't you ever get tired of expecting to die that way?"

"Gotta die somehow, and when it happens, I don't figure I'll really care too much about how it comes."

Sam looked at him, and a thought suddenly occurred to him. "Tell me something," he said. "With all this talk about prophecy and the Bible, do you believe in life after death?"

Long waited a moment, as the waitress brought their orders, but when she was gone, he nodded. "I do," he said. "When I learned about how accurate those prophecies are, I began to study them, and it hit me one day—how could there be a God who could inspire all of these people to write down these things that come true, and not be life beyond this world? Now, do I believe I'll go to Heaven? That's not something I'm willing to talk about, but yes, I do believe that it isn't over when our bodies die."

Sam watched him eat for a moment, and then dug into his own breakfast. They ate in silence, and a half hour later they were back on the road.

* * * * *

Harry Winslow lived in a nice neighborhood in Denver, in a house that he had bought not long after first moving to the city. He lived alone, having never married, and enjoyed his solitude to some degree, though he often wondered what life might have been like if he'd taken a less violent path. Now and then, a thought of Martha Lowenstein crossed his mind, and he wondered if she were still living. He hadn't seen her since they were both in college, and he'd made the choice to go into the Navy rather than ask her to marry him. By the time he'd become a SEAL and decided on a military career, she had dropped out and become a hippie, devoting her time to protesting the war in Vietnam and American politics in general.

Oh, well, those days were long gone, and he was sure she would have forgotten him many years before. He puttered around his kitchen as he usually did in the mornings, making himself some breakfast. On this particular morning, he chose oatmeal with cinnamon, since he needed the fiber, and had his usual single cup of coffee. He carried both of them to the table that sat just inside his back door, and dipped his head for a couple of seconds in the habitual grace he'd learned from his mother: "Thank you, God, for this day and its blessings." He didn't know if God was listening, but he figured it couldn't hurt to acknowledge Him in case He was.

At seventy-five years old, Harry was still in pretty good shape. He could still run an obstacle course that would leave many younger men gasping for breath, he maintained his black belts in five different martial arts disciplines, and he could still see and hear as well as ever. That was important to him, and he had his vision and hearing checked twice a year, just to be safe.

His phone rang, and he picked it up, expecting it to be Sam calling, but the number was blocked. He looked at the phone for two rings, and then answered it.

"Harry Winslow," he said.

"Harry!" came a voice through the line, and Harry thought it sounded familiar. A second later, he knew why. "It's Grayson Chandler, Harry, how have you been?"

Harry let himself grin widely enough for Chandler to hear it in his voice. "Why, I'm doing pretty well, Grayson, and yourself?"

"Not bad, not bad," Chandler said. "I hope I'm not interrupting anything; I just wanted to get in touch early this morning, see if maybe there's something about the David Glenn issue that you might want to talk about."

"David Glenn?" Harry asked. "Oh, that's the guy I asked about yesterday, isn't it? Is he one of yours?"

"Now, Harry," Chandler said, "we both know he is, and we both know why you're asking about him. I've taken the liberty of having both our lines scrubbed, so we can talk plainly. I'm hoping you'll tell me why you're suddenly so curious about Dave."

Harry smiled even wider. "Well, Grayson, I'll tell you," he said. "I've come across some intel that says he's been doing some unsanctioned wet work, and if he's one of yours, then I have to assume he's doing it for you. Considering the results of his actions, it sounds a lot like he's manipulating things to bring certain events to a head, and since those events are not in line with what I envision as the best interests of my country, I'm going to find out just what it is you're up to. Care to save me time and trouble, and just fill me in?"

Chandler laughed. "Harry, there's nothing to tell. Dave may have gone independent. From what I'm hearing this morning, he was told by someone last night that you were looking into his activities, and has disappeared. I think you scared him into hiding, Harry."

"Oh, well, then I'll just have to dig deeper, I suppose," Harry said. "Grayson, there's no point in beating around the bush, here. We're both pros at this, and we both know where it's going to end up, if we don't reach an agreement. If you can back off the program you're working on, I can back off the pressure I'm going to bring down on you. That way, you don't need to send your assassins after me, and I don't need to send any after you. Deal?"

Chandler was silent for a moment. "Harry, there isn't any program, and neither of us needs to send anyone after the other."

"Glad to hear that," Harry said, "but if there's one thing I learned about you Langley spooks while I was there, it's that the only way to tell if you're lying is to watch and see if your lips are moving. I've already got enough to tell me that they're moving now, because your program is pretty clear. Since you're lying about that one, I'm going to have to assume you're lying on the second part, and that you've already got someone ready to move on me." Harry sighed. "I shouldn't be too surprised, since I've already got someone coming after you, as well. I'm sure you remember Ken Long, don't you? He used to do some work for you now and then, surely you remember him?"

Chandler's silence, Harry knew, meant that he was carefully planning his next words. It also meant that he was trying to figure out a way to determine just how much Harry already knew and could prove.

"I remember Long," Chandler said, all the pleasantness gone from his voice and manner. "He went bad a few years ago, and I asked your people to ask you to bring him in. I guess you decided not to go there?"

"Well, we were going to, but then he sat down with one of my boys and told him some things that made us think maybe we should bring him in a different way—like to testify on Capitol Hill. Of course, that offer to put everything on hold still stands, though, if you want to take me up on it."

"Harry, you know, I'm regarded in DC as something of a fortune teller. It's amazing how often I can predict what's going to happen, so let me give you a little demonstration of my abilities, okay? One of two things is about to happen, and it's actually up to you to decide which one. Either Kenneth Long is going to show up on a police blotter with a bullet through his head, or you will. If you tell me it's going to be Long, then I'll expect to see a report to that effect within the next two hours. If not, then your corpse will be found sometime today. I've already got someone on you, Harry, so you can't avoid making the choice. Is this pathetic attempt at burning me worth dying over? Especially since I've got enough people hunting Long and your boy, Prichard, right now, to be sure that neither one of them ever gets to talk to anyone? Oh, and incidentally, I know they've left Denver, so I'm fairly sure they may be on the way here. Am I right about that?"

Harry laughed. "Grayson, don't threaten me. I've got my reasons for doing what I'm doing, and I'll see it through. Tell whoever you've got watching me to be sure they don't let me see it coming, will you? I'm tired, today, and I'd just as soon not have to kill anyone." He hung up the phone and leaned forward to eat his cooling oatmeal.

Eight minutes later, Harry Winslow rose and carried his bowl and spoon to the sink, rinsed them out, and put them into the dishwasher. When that was done, he went to his bedroom and began getting dressed for the day.

He heard the soft click of the back door as he was buttoning his shirt, and listened for the barely audible squeaks that came from the third and ninth steps on the stairs. When he heard the third step, he turned away from his dresser and went to the closet, opened the door and reached inside. He stood there, waiting, until he heard the ninth step, and then he withdrew his hand from the hidden shelf and produced the silenced Ingram machine pistol that he'd grasped, moving quickly to stand beside the large armoire that stood next to his closet door. That left him facing the doorway with a minimal profile, so when the two men burst into his bedroom with their own guns held out before them, all it took was one squeeze of the trigger to fire off a twelve round burst that struck them both through their heads. Both of them fell, and Harry lifted the barrel of his Ingram to point at the ceiling. He waited three minutes before moving, and then peeked around the bedroom door and down the stairs. No one seemed to be waiting there, so he looked back at the two men he'd just killed.

He didn't know either of them, but that wasn't a big surprise; there were so many new players on the field lately that he couldn't possibly know them all. Neither of them would be identifiable, of course; there would be no ID on them, and fingerprints and other forms of identification methodology would come up empty. He took out his phone and called his office.

"Ron? It's Harry. Listen, Son, I need a mop crew out at my house, ASAP. Got a little mess here that needs to be cleaned up. Yeah, two of 'em. Okay, I'll be in before too long." He cut off the call, then punched another quick dial icon.

"Hey, Harry," Sam said as he answered. "How's it going?"

"Well, I've got two dead men lying here bleeding all over my bedroom floor, and Grayson Chandler called this morning to tell me he was going to try to have me killed, unless I give him your friend, there. I declined, hence the need to have my carpet replaced."

Sam whistled. "Wow," he said. "I never would have guessed he'd try to take you out! Are you okay?"

"I'm fine, other than adding two more deaths to my conscience. Oh, wait, I don't have a conscience—I'm fine."

"Still, Harry," Sam said. "We must be onto something if he warned you and then tried to kill you. Can you use that against him? Show someone his call to you, and then the attempt on your life?"

"Not really, no. He didn't call on a line that would be provable, and there won't be any way to connect these men to him, that I can assure you. There isn't really any value in this, other than to let you know that you're definitely on the right track. I should probably thank him, because at least now we know for sure that he's the one behind the problems we're out to solve."

"Yeah," Sam said, "and from what Ken's been telling me, he may even be the Antichrist!"

9

Grayson Chandler was growing more and more anxious by the moment. He'd told Harry that he had people watching him, and even given him the courtesy of a warning, but he'd never have believed the old man could take out two of his best, not on his own. That seemed to be what happened, though, since neither of his men had checked in at the time appointed. The only reason they would fail to do so, he knew, would be if they were dead or captured, and these guys were pros; there was no way they'd allow themselves to be captured.

He'd called Harry from a blind phone while he was on his way in to the office that morning, and when Harry had refused to cooperate, he'd used the same phone to tell Mark and Lenny that they had the green light and a kill·order. They should have reported back to him within fifteen minutes that the old fart was dead, but it was now almost an hour later, and there was no word from them.

He was half surprised that Harry hadn't called him through his official line, just to gloat, but Harry was also a pro. He wouldn't even take the attack as an insult; it was just part of the job to a guy like him.

He checked the special monitors he'd installed, and verified that there were no eyes or ears installed in his office since the day before, then called Harry again on the blind.

"Hello?" Harry said.

"Harry," Chandler said. "You must be tougher than you look. I'm guessing my guys are dead?"

"Not at all," Harry said. "However, they're being skinned alive at the moment, so they're a little busy. I think one of them will be ready to talk to me fairly soon, and then perhaps we can get this all over and done with."

Chandler laughed. "Funny, Harry," he said. "If either of them was alive, you wouldn't be. Well, well, I guess I underestimated you. You can rest assured that I won't do so again."

"Then I can only assume your next shot will come from a distance? Grayson, let's cut to the chase, shall we? I'm not going to put myself in a position where you can get a shot at me, not for a few days, at least. You can still take my offer, and just shut things down. After all, you know I'm not going to let you succeed at what you're trying to do, so why not just sit back and enjoy your position?"

"Aw, c'mon, Harry," Chandler said. "You don't even

have a clue what it is I'm trying to do, so stop being coy. Give up Long, and nothing will happen to you or Prichard, but if you keep this up, I'm going to arrange your funerals, even if I have to set it up for after I'm gone. You know me, Harry, and I don't lose gracefully. Give me Long, get out of my way, and I'll be sure to remember and take care of you when this is all done. There could be worse things than having me owe you something this big, right?" Harry was quiet for a moment, and Chandler grinned. "Thinking it over, aren't you? C'mon, Harry, come in with me."

"I was thinking it over, that's true. The problem, Grayson, is that I absolutely do know what you're doing. You're trying to set yourself in a position that will make you indispensable to the head of the global government that you anticipate. Having you owe me a favor could be every bit as big as you say—except that I wouldn't want to be on the side of that global leader, so I don't want any favors from his right hand man. Read your prophecy, Grayson; you're treading a line that may not leave you a way out."

"Well, you surprise me, Harry. You're close, very close; and I happen to be very well read in prophecy, so I know exactly what line I'm walking on. We're coming to that time when everything comes to a head, and while some believe the Biblical predictions, there are other ways to interpret the events that will unfold. Why would I want to be anyone's right hand man, Harry, when I can be the one who's pulling the strings that control the puppet in the palace?" Chandler laughed again, and Harry felt something he hadn't known in fifty years, as a frisson of fear went down his spine. "You can't stop me, Harry, and if you really knew prophecy, you'd realize that already. The global power will come to be, and I intend to be well installed in the ceiling above it when it does."

Harry sighed. "Can we stop it? No, probably not, and I'm not sure we'd want to. On the other hand, if I'd met Hitler when he was a young corporal, and known what he would become when he rose to power, I like to think I'd have done everything I could to kill him, or stop him. If it turned out to be impossible, so be it, but I would have tried. Now you're asking me to look the other way while you become even worse than he was? Nah, Grayson, I have to oppose you, and if you don't back down, then I have to do all I can to stop you."

"As you say, then, so be it. I've tried to give you a way out, Harry. If you're going to be stubborn, then I guess I'll have to be ready for you. Take care, Harry; I won't miss again."

"Later, Grayson," Harry said. "I'm sure we'll talk again." He cut off the call, and then took out a handkerchief to wipe the sweat from his brow. For the first time in almost fifty years, Harry Winslow was afraid he might not succeed in carrying out the mission he'd set for himself.

In nineteen ninety-one, Harry had been introduced

to a man named Isaac Lambert, who was one of the eight-man panel who advised the President of the United States on the significance of biblical prophecy. Lambert had shown Harry various interpretations of what Christians call "end times" prophecy, including the rise of the Antichrist, the reformation of the Roman Empire (the ten horns), and the final battle that will take place at Armageddon when the world moves against Israel. Harry had been astonished at the impact of all this information, and had no doubt that the events they predicted would come to pass. Knowing that, he wasn't terribly surprised to find that someone like Chandler was trying to position himself to be near the top of that pinnacle of power.

Harry was scared, all right, because he had set himself a mission to try to thwart a man who may be the Antichrist, and since the Antichrist was part of prophecy, he just might not be stoppable.

He called Sam, who answered almost instantly. "What's happening, Harry?"

"Well, Sam, Boy, I think we've got a situation on our hands. I just talked to Chandler, and he's convinced he's going to pull this off. He's got himself set up in his mind as some sort of prophet of the new order, and I'm pretty sure he thinks he's actually destined to be at the head of the world government."

Sam had the phone on speaker, and Long said, "Harry—he's trying to set himself up as the Antichrist?"

"Actually, I don't think so," Harry said. "I think he's trying to be the false prophet."

* * * * *

Chandler wasn't afraid. He had accepted years ago that he was destined for this time and this position, and he had sought out the kind of advisers who could help him to plan it out. Bible prophecy experts came from many different schools of thought, and while there were certain parts of the prophecies on which almost all of them agreed, there were differing opinions on the final outcomes. Christianity claimed that after the battle to destroy Israel, Jesus Christ Himself would appear and reign on Earth for a thousand years, but other faiths saw things differently, and Chandler had found several that seemed to agree that the global empire would last forever, so that was the interpretation he chose to believe, and that was why he was doing all he could to put himself into the position of leadership of that empire. He had come to an understanding that led him to believe that the old Babylonian Gods were real and powerful, and devoted himself once a day to prayers to Shamash, the Sun God.

Shamash would be the God who would rule the world, and by aiding him in bringing his global rule to power, Chandler hoped to be his Regent here on Earth.

For now, though, he had to do some things the earthly way. He picked up his blind phone again and dialed a number, then waited for the woman who owed him favors to answer.

"Sandra? It's Grayson..."

* * * * *

Sam was driving, watching the Northern Indiana scenery slide by on either side of the Corvette. He'd been thinking for the past hour about the things Harry had said, and the more he thought about it, the more shaken he became. Finally he did the only thing he could think of, and called Indie.

"Hey, Baby," he said. "Just needed to hear your voice."

"Hey," she answered with a smile. "Sure is about time! How's it going?"

"Well, we're still on the road, and got a few hours to go before we get close to DC. We've decided not to go right into the city, because there are too many cameras; we're sure now that someone is anticipating us, so we don't want to be too easy to find."

"Okay," she said, "then be careful—and, Sam—oh, God, there isn't any other way to say it, but Beauregard wants me to give you a message."

Sam let out a sigh, and said, "Yeah, I had a feeling he might. Go ahead, I'm listening."

Indie took a deep breath. "Okay, here it is—he says you should listen for the Trumpet, because that's when you'll have to make your move. If you wait for the Trumpet, he says, then you'll stop the Great Evil, but if you don't, then you'll fail and the world will never be the same."

Sam Prichard drove his Corvette down the highway, and wondered why he'd been chosen to handle something that should have only been in the province of Preachers and Prophets.

He let his foot fall hard, and listened to the engine roar.

BOOK 7
DRIFTER: PART TWO

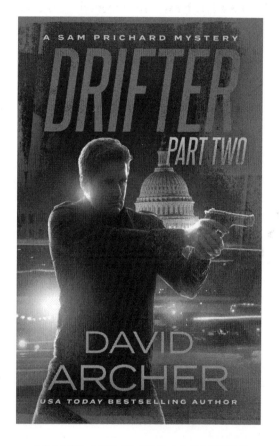

AVAILABLE ON AMAZON

ABOUT

David Archer was born and raised in Bakersfield, California. He is a fiction author and novelist, writing in the mysteries and thrillers genre. His approach to writing is to hit deep, keep you entertained, and leave you wanting MORE with every turn of the page. He writes mysteries, thrillers, and suspense novels, all of which are primed to get your heart pumping.

The author's books are a mixture of mystery, action, suspense, and humor. If you're looking for a good place to start, take a look at his bestselling Sam Prichard Novels, available now. You can grab copies in eBook, Audio, or Paperback on all major retailers.

Made in the USA
Coppell, TX
20 April 2020